HOOPER
FINDS A FAMILY
A Hurricane Katrina Dog's Survival Tale

By Jane Paley

HARPER
An Imprint of HarperCollins*Publishers*

Library of Congress Cataloging-in-Publication Data
Paley, Jane.
  Hooper finds a family : a Hurricane Katrina dog's survival tale / by Jane
Paley. — 1st ed.
    p. cm.
  Summary: Jimmy, a yellow Labrador puppy, is separated from his Lake
Charles, Louisiana, family and survives the horrors of Hurricane Katrina
on his own before being rescued and taken to New York City, where he tries
to fit in with a new family and the many neighborhood dogs, and accept his
new name.
  ISBN 978-0-06-201103-9
  1. Labrador retriever—Juvenile fiction. [1. Labrador retriever—Fiction.
2. Dogs—Fiction. 3. Animal rescue—Fiction. 4. Hurricane Katrina, 2005—
Fiction. 5. Survival—Fiction. 6. New York (N.Y.)—Fiction.] I. Title.
PZ10.3.P177Hoo 2011   2011002088
[Fic]—dc22   CIP
                                                                          AC

Typography by Tom Forget
11 12 13 14 15   LP/RRDB   10 9 8 7 6 5 4 3 2 1
❖
First Edition

For my boys

Contents

Chapter 1

Lake Charles

I smell salmon.

I bet Mamma's giving me some of last night's Sunday supper leftovers! I can't help myself; I have to scratch at the screen door so she'll hurry.

"Hold up, Jimmy. I have to get George's egg plate first."

I know, but I'm a puppy. It's hard for me to sit still when food's on the way. I press my face against the screen and drool into the little square holes.

It's about seven in the morning—that's when George has his egg plate and coffee. In a few minutes he'll be done eating. Then the door will squeak open and slam shut and he'll come out with my meal. While I have breakfast he'll sit in the metal rocker and smoke a cigar, because Mamma doesn't let him smoke in the house.

Here he comes.

"Morning, Jimmy. I got you some salmon today."

See? I knew it!

George and Mamma are my family. I'm their dog, Jimmy. We live in Lake Charles, Louisiana, not far from New Orleans. I've never been to New Orleans. Actually, I've never been out of our yard (well, except to go to the vet), but I heard George talk about New Orleans one time with Mamma. He had a job over there for a rich lady in a big house. George mows lawns and plants flowers and bushes for people with fancy gardens.

Every morning before the sun comes up, he waits on the porch for a truck to come and pick him up. That's when he gives me my breakfast. I never know what it's going to be. Sometimes it's corn and kibble with some bacon grease. Other times it's chicken, kibble, and carrots with a little egg from his plate. But whatever it is, it's always good.

Today it's salmon with greens and carrots, my second favorite. (I like roast beef the best and I always get the bone, which keeps me happy for a whole day.) Usually I'm gobbling up the last bites when a big truck rumbles up to the front gate. George always gives me a scratch and says, "You have a good day, hear?" before he heads off to work.

But today is different. There's no big truck. He's not going to work.

Mamma comes out and gives me a big bowl of ice cubes to chew on. I can't figure out how ice starts out crunchy and after a while turns into nice cold water. But I'm glad it does because I love to chew it. I crunch up little bits at a time so my teeth

2

won't hurt. Then I slurp up the chilled water and I lick the bowl while it's still cold.

I trot around the front yard, checking out the smells the night critters have left behind. Birds leave bits of food, feathers, and droppings on top of the lawn. Squirrels bury stuff. They think that my yard belongs to them. I don't trust those squirrels. They're sneaky. Any chance I get, I dig up something a squirrel has buried. The mice are not as bad, but they like to meet up under the porch, a space that also belongs to me. At least they have the sense to be afraid; the squirrels look right at me and dare me to chase them. Like that one. Right there.

Get lost, Bozo!

Nothing. He's twitching and scratching his ear. I crouch down low and stalk him. When I get close enough, he gets the message.

Ha! See that? He blinked and scurried up the old maple tree. I would have run him down, but it's too hot today.

When it cools off, I'll chase him right up to our neighbor's fence. That will annoy Kissy, the small white terrier next door. We are *not* friends. She barks for no reason. I bark when I have something to say, but not just for the sake of making noise. And her voice is not pleasant; it's kind of a high-pitched yap. Sometimes I bark over the fence and tell her to hush up, but it doesn't do a bit of good.

The front lawn is small, with a chain-link fence around it, so I never get very far from the house. The gate in the front is latched. But I can see the sights through the fence. I like to look at the neighbors' porches, where they play cards or watch the television or sit on their swings and listen to music, but today everything's different. Everyone seems to be leaving.

Mamma and George come out on the porch with two suitcases. Where are we going? I've never been anywhere before.

I get so excited I stumble over my big paws and then, whoops! I flop over. I bang my head on one of the legs of George's rocking chair. *Ouch!*

"Oh, Jimmy," says Mamma. "You just haven't grown into those feet yet, have you?"

Huh? My feet are right there, on the ends of my legs, like always.

"I don't like leaving him," Mamma says, looking down at me.

Leaving me?

"We can't take him to your sister's," George says. "You know how she is about dogs. I'll drop you off, and I'll come back and take him out to Jacob's farm. He'll be fine. Few drops of rain never hurt a dog yet."

"A few drops of rain!" Mamma snorts. "Man on the TV said the levees might break."

"Now, Mamma, quit worrying. I'll come right back for him."

I rush past them and sit by the gate, and whine a little to tell them to take me along. *I'll be good. Take me, please.*

Mamma sighs. She stops and pats me. Then she tells George to wait and runs inside. When she comes back, she's holding a nice beef marrow bone.

She gives it to me, and I'm so happy chewing I don't even watch Mamma and George get into the truck and drive away.

It's so hot that I have to take the bone into my hole in the front yard to keep cool. I've dug several holes, but this one is my favorite. I can see into the kitchen window if I look one way and keep an eye on the front gate if I look the other.

I gnaw on my new bone and think about burying it, but it tastes too good. I don't notice at first, but it's starting to sprinkle and it makes the yard steamy. I take my bone on the porch and crawl under a chair and go back to chewing. The thing about a big beef bone is that it lasts and lasts.

Now the rain is coming down harder. The ground is getting wet and cool. The dust in the air is clearing. I come out and roll around in the damp grass to give myself a back rub. Then I roll back over and nibble some of the wet grass. I'm not thirsty anymore.

The wind is picking up, and the sun has disappeared into the gray sky. This is perfect nap weather. I curl up with my bone between my paws. I'll work on it some more after a snooze.

Chapter 2

The Storm

It's hard to settle down and sleep. The rain keeps coming. And coming.

There goes Kissy again, yapping. She's begging to go inside, so her fur won't get wet. I don't understand girls.

I can hear the *poink poink* of the raindrops on the rain spout. The noise gets louder as the drops get bigger. I don't hear any more yapping; I guess Kissy's gone inside.

The drops are getting harder and the sky is dark. It sure is getting windy! I'd better move. Oops. Wait! I'll take my bone with me and it will keep me busy until the rain stops.

I head over to my special spot under the porch. There's a cracked board right where Mamma sits, and sometimes I sniff and tickle her toes from underneath. Now there are no toes to tickle, but never mind, it's nice and dry here.

But the rain starts leaking under the porch. This is not the best place to stay out of the rain after all. George said he was coming back for me. Where *is* he? He can't be out working on gardens in this weather. I'm whining, which I don't normally do, but nobody's around to hear me.

There's a puddle filling my spot under the porch, so I move up the steps and sit by the front door. It's getting windier! I think about watching the rain from inside the house because it's blowing too hard to sit outside. The shutters are clacking against the walls. Mamma left a window open and I can see the bottom of the red and white curtains blowing in and out. Suddenly, the screen door flies open and slams shut. *Bang!*

I jump about a mile and fly down the steps into the yard.

Hey! Quit doing that!

I have to find a safer spot. Maybe under a tree.

The bald cypress in the backyard has huge roots, and I snuggle in between them. I feel better until I remember my bone, so I dash back to the porch where I left it.

Clack clack! The shutters are slamming back and forth in a steady rhythm and the metal rocker is rocking, even though no one's sitting in it!

The laundry on the clothesline is spinning and spiraling in the wind. The legs of George's blue jeans are dancing! Then his shirt goes flying, and when it hits the ground it balls up and rolls toward the front of the house. The towels swing and fly away too, the blue, the blue stripe, and the big red one. They all end up pressed again the fence. It looks like everything's trying to run away from home except the underpants, which have curled tightly around the line. Finally, the clothesline snaps free of the metal ring on the side of the house and slithers off like a garden snake. Mamma sure will be angry when she sees this.

I run back to the tree with my bone firmly in my mouth.

I realize I'm getting soaked. My hiding place is useless. I go back up on the porch (but not near the screen door) and sit close to the wall where it's a little drier. I watch little streams gush into the holes I've dug in the yard. Mamma's tiny herb garden is flooding with rainwater. I wish she would come home. I'll wait right here by the door so she can let me in.

Leaves and twigs and bits of newspaper and dirty plastic bags are whirling in circles and blowing away. I've seen storms before, but this one is angrier than the others.

All of a sudden, there are huge zigzags of lightning across the sky. I've seen them before too, but never so many and such big streaks. The lightning flashes again and again, getting closer and closer until the storm is right over our house!

And then, a *gigantic* lightning bolt shoots straight down into the cypress. The one I was just sitting under!

There's a bang so loud it feels like it's right inside my head. And the next thing I know, I'm huddled under the porch again. I peek out to see what's happening.

With a crackle, the lightning spreads along the branches of the cypress; it looks like a tree all lit up for Christmas, but the twinkle doesn't last. Instead, each of the white lights bursts into a spray of sparks and smoke. And then the *whole tree* explodes!

Branches, leaves, chunks of bark, and most of the trunk blast off in every direction. I hear the side windows shatter. A shower of dirt, leaves, and twigs hits the porch, and dust and debris slide through the spaces between boards and cover me with mud.

I can't stay here! I leap from under the porch and run and run, but all I'm doing is making circles in the yard. I have to get over the fence!

I make myself slow down and stop. *Think, Jimmy, think.* And then I see it.

A huge chunk of the tree hit the fence when it fell. The chain link and one of the posts collapsed under it. That's my way out.

But the fence is hot and steam is rising up from it. It's also very slippery. I'm afraid of falling and getting stuck. Or getting fried! But I'm more afraid of staying here without Mamma or George.

I have to do a test. First I very lightly put a paw on the fence to see if it's still too hot to walk on. It's warm, but it doesn't hurt. I take a few careful steps.

Whoops! My back paw gets caught in the chain link. *Let go!* I gently shake my leg to get free and nearly lose my balance. But I stagger a few steps, and then I keep going.

Ouch! I've stepped on something sharp. I want to lick my paw, but I have to wait. *Keep moving, Jimmy.*

I make it past the fence and onto what used to be the street, which is now a shallow river. I sit down to lick the sore spot on my paw. It hurts a little but it's not bleeding. And then it hits me.

I've left the yard!

I've never been outside on the street, not in my whole life. It would be exciting, except for the rain pounding away and the rough wind that won't stop pushing.

I look up and down the street. The rain is so thick and hard, it's tough to see anything. I don't see George's truck. I don't see any cars at all.

I'm scared to move but I'm scared to stay still. I've got to go somewhere. I don't want to be by myself anymore.

Then I have a great idea! I'll go to Kissy's house! Somebody let Kissy in so someone is home there. Which way is it? I turn to look and the wind gets really rough and slaps me right into a bush. Whap! Leaves are whipping by and branches are scratching me and it seems to take hours to scramble and scrabble my way around.

Which way to Kissy's house? I'm getting all mixed up. But I catch a glimpse of her bright blue front door. I make a run for it.

I know I'm not supposed to scratch at doors. I whine a little, politely. I know I'm a guest and I should have good manners. But the door doesn't open.

So I bark.

It still doesn't open.

Then I forget about good manners and I bark, and I yelp, and I spring up on my back legs and claw at the door. *Hey, let me in! It's really scary out here! I'll be nice to Kissy, I promise.*

And then I see Kissy's face, at a window. She's yapping away, I can see her mouth opening and shutting, but I can't hear what she's saying. And I realize that if I can't hear her, nobody in the house can hear me.

There's another flash of white light, and another *BANG!* Before I realize what I'm doing, I'm running down the street.

Not running anywhere, exactly. Just running.

Chapter 3

The Flood

I run until the rain stops me. It's hard to run in this much rain. My feet are wet and cold and heavy.

There are no cars in sight at all. No lights, no people. Where have the birds gone? And the chipmunks and squirrels? Believe it or not, I'd like to see just one squirrel so I wouldn't be alone. I can't see any colors; just gray black.

I splash over to a wall and lean against it. I'm panting so hard. Need to catch my breath. I try to sniff for something familiar, but there's water where the air should be.

I can't see much, either. There are houses, but not my house with its broken chain-link fence. Not Kissy's house with the bright blue door. Those are the only houses I know. Everything is strange this far from home. I wish Mamma and George were here to tell me what to do. I'm just a puppy.

I can't even cry. The rain is blowing in my eyes. The wind is so loud I can't hear myself bark. The puddles have become ponds now. I can't see my paws anymore. When I look down, I see that the water is getting higher and higher. Pretty soon it's going to touch the fur on my belly.

The wind is pushing me from behind much faster than I want to go. But the water feels thick as I try to move through it. Changing direction is impossible, so I move along with the wind, fighting against the water. There's so much stuff blowing and swirling that I lower my eyes. But then I can't look around for shelter. I have to keep going and hope that someone will see me and let me into their house.

The water's brown and kind of sticky, and it smells like dead things, like the mouse that died under our porch one time.

There's no one to hear me, but it's worth a try. I bark. Wait. Did I bark? I didn't hear myself. I try again, but the wind is much louder. I don't think any sound is coming out.

I think I've lost my bark.

I feel so little and weak.

How will I ever get back home?

I know what I have to do—go up higher. Then this water won't be able to drown me. I'll climb high up, away from the water, and then I'll figure out how to get home when the rain stops.

There's a little hill off in the distance. I start toward

it—walking, this time. I'm too tired to run.

But the current is going against me, and it's strong. It's pushing and pushing.

I put my head down. I growl. I strain to move forward.

One step. Then another.

The water's getting deeper. Nobody ever told me how *hard* it is to walk in deep water!

It's covering my legs and it's almost up to my chest.

There's got to be a better way. I start to paddle because the ground is getting farther away from my feet. This is different from walking. There's a rhythm to it, like the beat of a song. And suddenly I'm not walking anymore.

I'm swimming!

I never knew I could swim. My feet are gliding and I can raise my head enough to see the hill. I can breathe more easily too. There's a pattern to breathing and paddling. I wouldn't mind doing this on a nice day, but this is the worst day ever to be learning how to swim!

I'm still not making progress toward that little hill. The water's in charge, and I'm just going where it wants to take me. We sail around trees and mounds of branches and lumber from houses and porches. I stretch my head up and keep pumping my legs so the current won't suck me under. I hope I don't get clobbered by a hunk of wood or a—

Hey, that hurt!

The water's slammed me up right against a telephone pole, banging my ribs. I yelp with the little breath I've got left and dig with my claws, trying to catch hold of it and slow myself down. But the pole is wet and slippery, and before I can figure out what to do I'm swimming again. Only now I hurt, and it's harder to keep my nose out of the water.

The water boosts me up a little, over something underneath (what is it, a rock? A curb?) and then suddenly, without warning, it pulls me under and into a spin.

I can't breathe! I can't breathe down here!

The water's in my mouth and it tastes horrible. There's no sound. Everything is murky and brown, but I can see some light. I struggle toward it, all four of my paws working like mad. My head pops out and I grab the air—

And I go under again.

And again.

I only have time for quick breaths. Every time my nose and mouth poke out of the water, I only have a second before it closes over my head again. I'm confused and dizzy and I don't know which way to swim. I whirl around and around. I'm drowning in water and mud. I twirl and swirl faster now. It feels hopeless.

But it's not. There's something down here with me. Ow! It jabs and thumps into me. My front paws grab hold and hang on long enough to look around.

My face breaks through the water. I can breathe again! But who knows for how long?

I blink; my eyes are still full of water. But I kick and climb and scramble onto whatever it is. I shake my head so hard my ears flap back and forth. Finally, I can see.

It's a tree trunk. I'm holding on to a tree trunk! It's got branches and roots and leaves, and I'm hanging on to the muddy, slimy tangle of roots. It's impossible to climb it. My feet keep getting caught and then slipping out from under me. It's wobbly and I don't feel safe. I'm crouched down and digging all of my claws into the muck. I'm still in the water, but at least I can stop swimming for a spell.

I sneeze and wheeze and cough up stinky water and taste gritty dirt and sand on my tongue. I want to get up on top of the trunk, but how?

It's no use. I can't. I don't have the strength to fight it anymore. I don't have the strength left to do *anything*.

My back paws are kicking in the water and I'm losing my grip in the front.

Plosh! I fall backward and tumble under again. I'm completely submerged except for my eyes and nose.

"Hey, *psst*. Over here."

Huh? What was that?

I look up and see an otter nodding at me from above.

What's he so calm about?

"You're on the wrong end. See? This side has a big limb you can straddle."

I'm gasping and panting.

"Ride the current; don't fight it. You won't win."

I stop thrashing and float. I see what he means. I bump and slap against the side of the tree until I reach his end. I struggle to crawl onto the thick limb he's resting on, but keep falling backward.

"Easy! You're fighting with the water again. Let the current help you."

I'm not sure what he means. After a bit, I feel the water pushing me! I put my front legs over the trunk, kick my back legs, and wiggle my behind.

Uh.

I pull and I heave and I'm almost there. This is hard work! But he's right. I finally get out of the current and onto the fat part of the trunk. I shake as much water from my coat as I can without losing my balance.

"Thanks."

The water is crashing past us.

"Where am I?"

"You're in a storm, ding-dong."

"No, I mean—"

He chuckles, and then without a splash or even a ripple, he's disappeared under the water.

Where'd he go?

I teeter on the tree trunk, and I know that any minute I'm going to slip back in. I get my breath back and look around.

The otter's head bobs back up.

"Over there," he chirps.

He's happy, for Pete's sake.

"Over there what?"

"A safer spot for you to wait out the storm!"

A surge drives me right back into the water and I try to ride the current again. But the top of the water is moving in a different direction than the bottom, so I start to twist in circles. I give up. The otter is right. I won't win. I'm gurgling water out of my nose and losing my bearings. I go round and round until I can't tell the sky from the sea. The water is churning me so fast that I shut my eyes and give in. The next thing I know, I've slammed into something else and I can feel that it's hard and solid. It's steep. I press my paws against it. The hill!

"That's it. Up you go!" the otter calls out. "See?"

Ohhh. I do see.

I climb with my front paws and kick my hind legs. The water keeps trying to drag my back feet away, but I won't let it. I try and try to heave myself up. The surface of the hill has ridges, and I cling to them with my nails.

Wait a minute! This isn't a hill. It's a roof! It's not as big as our house; it's some kind of shed. And it's a way out of the water.

Chapter 4

The Roof

I keep climbing slowly, so I don't lose my footing. I stumble and backslide, but catch myself before I fall back in. A bit farther up, there's a window with a little flat shelf. Probably there used to be a window box on it, like the one outside our kitchen.

I crawl up to it slowly, reminding myself that it's better to move carefully than to rush. The otter is right; the storm is strong and I am not. I have to fight the sharp angle of the roof against the wind, which is still raging.

Finally I get there and collapse. The little shelf is just wide enough for me to lie down. It's full of mud and leaves. I shake my head to get the water out of my ears. That helps. I want to thank the otter, but he's vanished.

I don't look at the water; I want it to forget about me. I look up at the sky, like Mamma does sometimes. I hear her say,

"Thank you for another day." I feel better now just thinking about that.

I stay on the shelf. The water is racing past my roof, and branches, roots, and big clumps of earth are spinning by. Chunks of stuff smack into whatever gets in the way. I see a chair like the one on our porch, a tire, and a dead animal whirling around and around. I'm not sure what it is, but now I'm afraid and sad at the same time. The whole floor of the world is moving, and I press myself hard against the window so I won't be swept away, too.

I'm *really* thirsty. I think I'm more thirsty than I am hungry. I lick the raindrops off the window behind me and suck up the tiny puddles that have formed in the corner of the windowsill. But it's not enough.

Just below the window box is a ridge running the width of the shed. It's like the gutters on George's roof. Now and then, George gets up on a ladder to clear out the leaves so the rain can run off the roof into a barrel. This ridge has ribbons of clean rainwater and if I lean down far enough I can lick them up. I stretch as far as I can to lap up what's right below, but there's more water in the corner. Quite a lot of water, in fact. But getting close enough without falling over is a big challenge.

I really need some water. I haven't drunk anything since I had those ice cubes Mamma left me. You can't count that filthy water that got into my nose and mouth when I was swimming, since I coughed it all back up.

I stare at the puddle in the corner below. Finally I can't

take it anymore. I inch forward off the shelf, gripping the shingles as tightly as I can with my nails.

Careful, Jimmy, careful. You can do this!

I go slow. Inch by inch, I make it down to the puddle. I stick out my tongue and drink.

Oh, that's good.

It's not enough, but it's way better than nothing. I lick up every drop. Now comes the hard part: to get back into my little shelter in the window box, I have to back up. It's too sloped to turn around. It's just a few steps backward. My back legs shake as I rear up two steps. One. Two.

I make it! I'm proud of myself. I was careful and I didn't slip once.

It grows darker. But no matter how tired I get, I can't sleep. I'm still so thirsty. And now I'm getting hungry. I think about my bone. I guess I left it back in the yard. I wish I had it with me. Maybe if I wish hard enough it will appear, just like that, between my paws.

It doesn't.

Where is everybody? Where is anybody? I need somebody to bring me another bone. And a dish of water. And salmon with a little baked potato. Or some bacon with George's left-over scrambled eggs! What happened to the people who live here? Are Mamma and George safe? Did our house drown like this one? I'm even worried about Kissy, and I *never* worry about Kissy.

And there's another reason I can't fall asleep—I can *hear*

things. Lots of things. I can hear the rain hitting the water—*splip, splip*—and I can hear it hitting the roof—*thonk, thonk, thonk.*

I can hear the wind howling and I want to howl back, but I'm too scared to move. I hear sirens in the distance. They're howling at the wind instead of me.

Sometimes I think I hear voices. But they're far away. I can't tell what words they are saying. It sounds like someone is crying. I feel like crying, too. I whimper along. This is a long, sad night. Maybe the storm has washed all the days away.

I squint and sniff the air. There are humans! And they're headed in my direction.

Hey! Over here! Come get me!

Far away, in the mist, is a boat. It's not a big boat, but it has a motor that sounds like George's truck.

George? Mamma? Can you see me? I try to stand up so I'll look bigger.

I want to make noise, but all that comes out is a baby squeak. Where's my bark when I need it?

The boat is getting closer. I can make out some people in it. I see a man. George?

I'm so happy you're here!

Wait! There's a man, but it's not George. And in the front—wait! It's a dog! They get closer and I realize it's another family, not mine. There's a mom and what looks like two children. From this far away, I can't tell if they're boys or girls.

The woman is sitting with one child in her lap and one

snuggled up next to her. The dog is big. A German shepherd.

Those people can come and get me! They'll take me back to Mamma and George. Yes! Yes!

"Doggie! Doggie!" It sounds like a little girl saying it and pointing at me. They can see me! I don't have to bark after all! But the German shepherd has different ideas. He lets loose a dark warning growl.

Hey, I'm friendly. I just need a ride home.

"Can we pick up the puppy?" The little girl begs. "Pleeease."

"No, sugar." It's a man's voice, deep, like George's. "We can't fit him. There's barely enough room in this boat for us and Rufus won't like it."

Rufus gives me an unfriendly stare, then looks straight ahead toward the lights in the distance.

"But Mommy, the puppy will die."

"No, he won't, darling girl. There's land just over there. See? By morning he'll be able to wade over."

And then the boat is gone in the mist. I'm all alone again.

But wait! There's land right over there, where the red and yellow lights are. I can make it by myself. The storm is quieting, and soon it will be safe to climb out of the window box.

Chapter 5

Alone

I look up at the sky. Everything is still. There is complete silence. No birds are singing; no dogs are barking. Sirens have stopped wailing and there are no sounds of boats. I hear myself breathing.

The sky slowly clears. The water is slapping the side of the house, but not very hard. I'm not sure, but I think the water is lower than it was before. Yes! It's definitely not as deep.

Hooray! The storm is over! There is a beautiful calm around me, and the black air has turned to gray fog. I lick some of the mud off my coat. If the storm is over, it means I'll be going home soon. And I want to look good for Mamma.

But there's something wrong with the silence. It's too quiet. Should I make a dash for the land now? It's too foggy to see the red and yellow lights. I don't know which way to go anymore. I should have gone last night. I could have followed right behind the boat.

I startle when I hear a loud rumble, and I have to hang on so I don't slip down the roof. *Careful, Jimmy! Don't ruin things now!*

I look up. The sky is getting dark again.

Soon there's no hint of light, no moon, no stars, *no sky*. Just heavy, thick, swirling clouds. The rain is coming down hard again. Harder than before. And the winds are speeding up. I was wrong. The storm isn't over.

A gust of wind whips through treetops, unleashing clouds of leaves and branches. I hear the sound of something creaking and groaning, but I can't tell where it is.

Then I see it. Out on the water, but moving fast. It's another roof! A gigantic one! But this one isn't attached to a house. It's just sailing on the water, and it's coming closer and closer and—

Crash!

It hits *my* roof, and when it does, a wave of dirty, smelly water swooshes over everything. Before I know it, I'm swirling in a wild rush of water. I get caught in branches and leaves and pulled under.

Hunks of wood are slamming into me and I can't get any air. I'm in *big* trouble.

The floating roof, which is in front of me, crashes into a clump of trees and stops! This may be my only chance to get out of the raging waters.

I try to crawl on top of the roof, but I slip and tumble

25

backward. I can get my front paws on the edge, but I can't pull myself up. So I hang on.

I can't do this forever. And when I slip off, I'm pretty sure I won't have the strength to swim anymore.

I hold on tight, remembering the otter's advice: Don't fight. I wait for the right moment when the water's on my side. Maybe I can get a boost when it shifts direction.

And then I see it. Slithering along the roof. Long and dark and shiny, it slides slowly in my direction. I've seen snakes before, but most of them curl up in the rocks or in hollows of trees. They only get mad if you bother them. But this one means business. He slinks closer and coils close to my head.

Hunger

"Thisssss isssss mine," the snake hisses.

Oh no. I'm in his territory. But I have no place else to go.

He pulls his head back and opens his mouth wide. It's white inside. That's how I know he's a cottonmouth, the most dangerous snake in all of Lake Charles. George knows all about them from working in gardens along the lake. I look at his fangs; I do not want to get bitten. I crash back into the water, which right now looks better to me than an angry snake. The snake glides into the water and moves alongside me. What's he doing?

I struggle while the snake curls through the water with ease. What does he want from me? I'm too big to eat, aren't I? I don't look at him, but I can hear his hissing. He stretches out each word.

"Ssssssad, sssssorry sssswimmer, you are."

I am, but right now I'm panicky that I'll be ssstung.

He's mocking me.

"Sssstupid ssspecies."

I peek up in search of another resting spot. Way up in the sky, I see a bird circling. He's hovering high above my head, wings spread wide. I can't tell what he's up to, but I think he's spotted me. Then I realize he's not any old bird; he's a hawk.

A hungry hawk.

The snake is hissing and I keep looking up at the first hawk I've seen since the storm started. Each time he circles, he drops lower in the sky.

Suddenly, he tucks his wings into his body and dive-bombs down out of the sky straight at me. If I could swim underwater I would, but I have no idea how and no time to come up with another plan.

So long, Jimmy!

It happens so fast. I see the hawk just long enough to watch his sharp, curved claws open and scoop up the snake, writhing silently in his tight grip. After that, all I can see is the shadow of his wings as he swoops back into the sky, flapping hard.

Did this really happen? First I thought the snake would bite me, then I was sure a hawk would attack me, and now, here I am, waterlogged, lost, and hopelessly sinking in foul floodwaters.

I get it. The rain has let up, and all the animals that have survived the storm are hungry.

I'm getting very hungry too.

Chapter 7

More Trouble

I drift back to the flat roof now that the snake is gone. I wait for a surge and hoist myself up on the first try! The roof keeps me above the water, like a raft. But there's no window with a little shelf for me.

The otter bounces up out of the water and smiles.

"You're getting it. Now, move to the middle of the raft. You'll have better balance there. See?"

I crouch down low and move to the middle. I spread all four legs out as far as they will go. And I *hang on*.

I liked my old roof better. It didn't move under me. This one does. It shakes and quivers as the water pulls at it. It's staying where it is, for now, jammed into the clump of trees, but the water keeps slapping, and sometime soon I bet it'll tug this roof loose.

Then where will I be? Twisting around in the water again.

Until I bang into something else.

"Don't be glum, chum," chirps the otter again as he swims off. "You'll be okay!"

But I don't feel okay. I wish the otter would keep me company. It's lonely out here. If only those people had room in their boat. I would have been a very polite passenger. But there's no point in thinking about something that didn't happen. I have to figure out what's next.

I know what the otter has told me, but I need to explore. A big bunch of branches is stuck. Maybe if I can get up over there, I'll have more protection from the rain.

I wobble unsteadily, trying to keep in rhythm with the rocking of the raft. I slip and roll sideways, and I snag my back leg on something sharp.

Ouch!

I twist around to look. My leg is bleeding. A nail sticking up from a shingle must have cut me.

I lick the cut until it feels better. Then, little by little, I creep so that I'm sheltered under the branches that hang over my new home.

This is a better spot. The rain doesn't hit me quite so hard here. And some of the leaves are catching the raindrops, so I can lick them off. I do. They taste good and quench my thirst.

And then I smell something even better than wet leaves. I raise my head and sniff. *Food!*

It's not kibble or beef or salmon, but it smells familiar. It's coming from the edge of the raft. I inch over very slowly so I don't lose my balance.

Look at this! The remains of a nest are caught in some twigs, and there are baby birds in the bottom. I can't believe how lucky I am.

Now, how am I going to get to them?

The nest is tangled in a mesh of branches beyond the raft and just out of reach. I'll need to lean over the side to get to it. This means I have to take a chance that I'll fall back into the water. It's also very windy. I could get to the nest and get caught in the branches. Then I'd be back in the water again. It's a big gamble, but I'm so hungry.

I inch closer and closer. Just as I'm getting near enough to see into the nest clearly, I hear something vibrating. For a second it sounds like George snoring. But the snore explodes into a snarl. Then a deep, harsh rumble. Then a scream. It's the meanest sound I've ever heard in my whole life and it's right above my head in a tree.

Whatever it is must want the birds for itself. I'm not the only one who's really hungry. I know better than to start a fight with something that sounds as powerful as this does. The sound stops for a moment. Maybe it was growling at someone else. I stay very still.

But then it starts up again. This time it's louder and closer. I try to back away from the nest without turning around, but the best I can do is turn away. As I move, I can feel the creature moving with me. I peek up without moving my head and I see it on a branch a few feet above me.

It's a cat. I've seen them before. But it's not a kitty cat.

Uh-oh. *A bobcat.* I can see his glowing yellow eyes, unblinking, fixed on me. His nose is quivering, then he draws his lips back tightly over his gums into an evil smile. It's not a smile at all. And he's not looking at the birds. He's locked on me.

I understand.

He doesn't want to eat the birds.

He wants to eat *me.*

He hunches over, his back humped, his neck stretched out, his mouth watering. Droplets of spit are hanging from his fangs.

There's only one way I can escape. I roll back into the water and actually feel relieved to be swallowed up by waves again. I wonder if he'll dive in and devour me; I know bobcats can swim. I hope for the best. I've hit the water with a big splash. Maybe I splashed him away. I look up and see the leaves rustling. The bobcat is leaping through the branches in another direction!

Phew. That was *really* close.

Struggling to stay afloat, I remember the otter's advice again; I try not to fight the tide. I hang on to the side of the raft and pedal my legs slowly. Just enough to tread water, but not enough to go anywhere. I scan the treetops and I don't see the bobcat. I look around for snakes and don't see any. But you never know. Another one could slide out of the water anytime and sink his poison into my empty little belly.

I wonder if the baby birds are still there. My heart is beating fast, but I feel a tiny bit proud of myself. I didn't get eaten!

But now what? I'm even hungrier than I was before. I want those little birds. Do I dare climb back up on the raft and make my way back to the nest?

"Are you in the water *again*?" the otter wants to know as he pops his head to the surface. "Not too smart, are you?"

"I'm smarter than a bobcat," I tell him.

"Bobcat?" He sounds worried. "Gotta go."

Before he dives, he points me to the most accessible part of the raft and I wiggle my way back onto it. I'm sore from all this climbing and scuttling, but I stay focused on the possibility of a meal. If I don't eat something soon, I think I'll have to give up.

Is the otter a mind reader? He springs out of the water and adds, "Whatever you do, don't give up!"

He's right, Jimmy.

Once again, I grab the ridges in the roof and pull myself onto the far end of the raft. I keep looking up to see if the bobcat has come back for me. I'm not going to know for sure until I hear him growl because he moves so silently and gives no advance notice of his plans.

I get near enough to see the nest, but the raft is rocking close and then retreating away from it. I have to time my move very carefully. I lie as close to the edge as I can with my head and front legs dangling over the water. I drift closer, but I can't move fast enough.

My tummy is talking. *Feed me.*

Each time I get within range, I lose my nerve. Finally, when the time is right, I thrust my face into the nest, but not fast enough to grab a bird. I try again and nearly slip into the water.

Okay. This time, I'm going to do it.

I stop thinking about missing or falling or looking around for the bobcat and I go for it. I lean over and snatch one. While the raft is rocking, I gobble it up. It's so good, I grab a second bird without hesitating.

Oh boy.

I have a full tummy, and I think I'm going to be okay. I can stay here for a while. And the rain will stop. It has to stop sometime.

So that boat didn't stop for me. So what? Soon Mamma and George will come to get me. Or the water will go away, all by itself, and I'll just jump down and walk home. There will be a yummy meal waiting for me: salmon, and chicken, and of course a big roast beef bone. And Mamma will pet me and tell me how brave I was during the storm, and how smart I was to get away from that bobcat, and what a good boy I am to find my way home.

I'm thinking about all those things, and I start to relax. I stretch out on the roof and doze off. I didn't really sleep last night, after all. And there's nothing to do but sleep while I wait for Mamma and George to come and get me.

I dream about Sunday afternoons. George's friends are watching the baseball game, whooping and laughing. Mamma is humming her tunes. I'm gnawing away on my beef bone. It's a really good dream.

When I wake up again, I can't tell how much time has passed. Somewhere in the distance I hear a new sound and pick up the scent of humans.

Something is slapping the water in a steady rhythm. *Slap, slap, slap.*

It's Mamma and George! I have to let them know I'm here waiting!

I bark. I bark again, but I'm not making any sound. Nobody comes, and if somebody could hear me, they'd come, right?

I think back to the last time I tried to bark and I couldn't hear myself. The storm hasn't just taken me away from home. It's taken my bark away. What kind of a dog can I be without a bark?

I peer out through the rain.

I see it! But what is it?

It's definitely headed this way. Oh, look! A man in a yellow hooded raincoat is paddling toward me. I have to make enough noise so that he'll hear me. No bark comes, so I let out a big cry.

Please, please help me. I'll be a good boy.

He's squinting in my direction. He looks around.

Over here.

OVER HERE!

Chapter 8

The "Boat"

He spots me! The man sees me!

He rows over to my roof and shouts, "I'm coming!"

Oh, thank you, thank you!

He's not in a boat. He's on a door that he's made into a raft! It looks just like our front door, with a doorknob sticking out! And look at this! He's paddling with a broom! He strokes on one side, then flips the broom to the other to keep moving straight in my direction.

He's just a few feet away now. "C'mere, little fella," he calls.

He seems to want me to do something. What?

He's beckoning with his hands, like Mamma does when she wants me to come and play. He puts the broom down and pats his knees.

Finally I get it. He wants me to jump!

Jump? No way!

His raft is close, but it's rocking and shifting side to side. If I don't make it, I'll be in the water again.

I don't want to go back, thank you very much!

"You can do it, fella," the man says.

No, I can't. I'm too clumsy. Mamma always said I was the clumsiest pup she'd ever seen.

The man steadies his little raft by leaning over the front, stretching out his arms, and grabbing my big raft with both hands.

"Jump, little fella, or I'll have to leave you here," he says.

Leave me?

Those other people left me. They saw me but they wouldn't come to get me. I'm way more scared of being left here all on my own than I am of jumping. I leap up and hurtle down onto his makeshift boat, my feet slipping and my legs flying in every direction. I launch myself right at him. He tries to grab me and I knock him over flat. He lands hard. The boat rocks and sways, and the broom falls into the water.

"Whoa, whoa!" he says. "You're the clumsiest dog I ever saw. You're going to spill us both right into the water!"

He leans over and grabs the broom just in time. *I'm sorry.* I stare sadly up at him. *I didn't mean to.*

"Okay!" He rubs my ears. "Don't worry. Lie down and stay flat." I do—with a splat. I start to wag my tail. First it just twitches. Then back and forth, slowly.

"We're plain lucky I had a door and a broom handy," he says as he slowly rows toward dry land. "Sometimes when you don't have what you need, you use something else."

I understand him. When there's no food bowl, you have to swallow up baby birds.

"Don't worry, partner. I'll take you somewhere safe."

My tail picks up speed. Somewhere safe! At last! This man is going to take me home. I'll see Mamma and George and my beef bone and my holes in the yard. I'm even looking forward to seeing Kissy again! I'm going back to my yard and I'm never, ever going to leave it again!

I'm so happy I sit up and thump my tail hard. The door wobbles under me. It's even shakier than my second roof!

"Whoa, partner. Don't tip us in."

Oh. Okay. I guess I can be happy and lie still. But my tail won't settle down. It just goes smack, smack, smack.

The man rows our raft toward a line of trucks in the distance. Land again. Yay! The raft hits dirt and lurches to a stop. My rescuer picks me up. I let him hold me. I look around for home.

That's strange, I don't see Mamma and George's house. There's a fire truck, an ambulance, and another big truck. The back doors are open and I see cages.

Cages?

Wait! I don't like cages! I want to stay with you until I get home.

"Sorry, partner," the man says. "I see you don't like it, but you've got to go in. It'll be okay, I promise."

You promise? From the moment the door of the truck slams

shut, there is chaos. The cages are cramped and the smells of pee and panic are everywhere. But I don't howl like the rest. I lie down quietly and lick my muddy paw pads until they are pink again.

"They're taking us to the death house!" a mutt in the corner shrieks.

Everyone is howling and crying. "It's worse than a death house," a cat mewls back. "You'll *wish* you were dead when you get there."

The old spaniel in the next cage wheezes, "It's NOT a death house. It's a safe house from the storm."

It's no use. Everybody believes the death-house story and yowls.

I refuse to believe any of it.

"Are they driving us to our homes?" I ask the old guy, who's wheezing so loud I wonder if he'd make it out of the van at all.

"No, boy. You'll never see your home again."

Never? He's wrong. George and Mamma will be looking for me and I'll wait patiently until they arrive. I'm not falling for these horror stories. George promised to come home for me, but instead he'll look all around until he finds me. But as the truck bumps along and the stench of pee and wet fur overwhelms me, I'm not as sure.

"I've heard that they starve dogs there if no one comes for them," a dog in the front murmurs, but we can all hear him.

"Shut up!" a clipped poodle squeals. I can tell she's just like Kissy, spoiled and pampered.

It's getting hotter and smellier, and the old spaniel can't breathe. "He's gonna die!" the cat nearby screams.

I look over at the old spaniel and whisper, "Shhh. Take slow breaths. Don't try to talk. We'll be there soon and they'll give you medicine." He closes his eyes and I watch to see if his chest is rising and falling. When we get there and the back doors open, he doesn't move.

A man and woman unload us one by one.

"Oh look," the woman says. "This poor guy didn't make it."

"See?" the cat hisses snidely. "I told you he'd die."

I can't believe what I'm seeing and hearing. I'm getting more worried that maybe, just maybe, I'm never going to see George and Mamma again.

But then I change my mind. That spaniel was wrong. I'll get back home again, somehow.

Chapter 9

The Shelter

Two men take the old spaniel away, carrying his cage between them. And then, one of the men comes back for me. He carries my cage, and a lady carries the nasty cat.

"I'm worried sick about my kids," she says. "They're at a Red Cross facility waiting to hear about their house."

"I've got room in my place; they can come stay with me."

I want to listen to more of what they're saying. Maybe I can find out about George and Mamma. But the man puts me in a cage and shuts the door with a cold metal *click*.

This cage is bigger than the one in the truck, and there's a metal bowl full of water. But it's still a cage, and it smells of a cleaning product. It's like the kind Mamma uses sometimes, but much stronger. It burns my eyes and nose.

Is this really a death house? I can't believe that these people—who are bringing us here and giving us shelter and water—would go to the trouble if they didn't intend to take us home. Of course that's what's going to happen. They're going to scoop us up one by one and take us home if our families don't come for us. But first they have to figure out who we belong to. I take a long drink.

Ahh. Much better.

As horrible as this place is, I calm myself thinking about home.

I look at the cage across from mine. There are three small dogs, a beagle and two mutts. They're all the same size and I wonder if they're together because they all come from the same family. I'm alone because I'm an only dog. The beagle is howling and the mutts are facing me, but they don't really see me. They look far away and sad. They don't seem like friends.

Suddenly my cage opens and a scruffy dog swaggers in. He has one good eye; the other is sewn shut.

"Hello," I say politely.

He shoves past me roughly and slurps up the water in my bowl.

Hey! I wasn't finished with that!

He glowers at me and mutters something I don't hear. I don't have to. I know whatever he said was unfriendly.

I decide it's best if I leave him alone, so I lie down in the spot farthest from him.

"Move," he growls. "That's my spot."

I don't want to fight, so even though it's a tight squeeze, I move over.

"Move," he repeats in the same nasty tone. "That's my spot."

What? I just gave him the spot he wanted.

He growls a little louder.

Oh, all right. I move again.

This dog looks like he's been in more than a few fights, and I don't want to be in his next one.

But before he gets a chance to push me around another time, the door of our cage swings open and someone shoves a bowl of dry food in. It turns out this dirty, straggly, one-eyed dog has no trouble seeing the bowl; he bolts over to it and digs in. He takes enormous bites, and each time I try to get my face in, he slams into me without missing a morsel.

I run to the other side of the bowl. I get around him but only manage to get two or three little bites before he's devoured the whole bowl. This is not fair. He eats so much faster. If this goes on, I'll starve. Didn't one of the dogs in the truck say something about that?

I'm so hungry.

But my food fight is tame compared to the three dogs across from us.

They scuffle and snarl when their bowl comes and the two mutts attack the beagle as soon as he starts eating. Then the three of them crowd together and eat so frantically that they push the bowl around the cage until they've licked it clean. Along the way, a little kibble spills out and the two mutts wrestle for it.

It seems to get quieter while the dogs along the rows eat, but soon the crying and yipping and yowling echo loudly in the cement hallways. This is a miserable place.

People walk by, collecting the food bowls and refilling the water. One-Eye growls at them. He also growls when new dogs come in, and he lunges at a collie when she accidently brushes past our cage. "Shut up!" he roars at her for no reason.

Nobody comes to give *us* water. I wonder if they're afraid of One-Eye.

I don't know what to do. He's so angry at everything.

"Do you want this spot?" I ask him in a tiny voice.

"What? Huh?"

"I want to lie down."

He scratches himself and looks away.

"Lie down wherever you want."

Maybe my good manners have calmed him down a bit. He stops growling and lies down too. But he doesn't close his one good eye. He watches everything.

"Aren't you tired?"

"Can't get tired. Have to watch for trouble."

At that exact moment, the cages start opening and some of the dogs charge down the hall. Cage after cage opens and when it's our turn, we follow the dogs out to a yard.

On the way I notice that not all the dogs leave their cages. Some cower in the corners, afraid to leave. Some cry and move slowly, trying not to get mowed down by the faster dogs. Still others can't decide whether to go or not, so they hover.

When we get to the doorway I understand why.

The gravel yard is filled with dogs. Big setters, medium mutts, tiny poodles, hounds of all sizes, and retrievers like me. Some run wildly; others have best friends and play together alone. A few charge at dogs that get in their way, daring them to fight. I stand stock-still, too frozen with fear to go in.

"Don't look weak," One-Eye whispers gruffly, "or they'll come after you."

I edge in, but I don't look at any dogs. I don't want them to think I'm interested in fighting.

"You!" One-Eye snarls loudly at a much bigger dog than he is. "You want trouble? I'll give you trouble."

The big dog gallops off, but a gray terrier bounds over and snarls right back at him.

"Okay, I'll take your trouble and give you some back."

I can't believe what I'm seeing. One-Eye has challenged every dog in the yard and he has a taker! A feisty little terrier. A *dumb* feisty little terrier.

The terrier is smaller, but he's mighty vicious.

He and One-Eye go at it and the terrier takes a bite out of One-Eye's shoulder. But One-Eye lunges and sinks his teeth into the terrier's throat and flips him onto his back.

One of the shelter workers bursts into the middle of the yard, waving a gun. He points it at One-Eye.

Before I can think twice, I rush into the fray and screech (because I still can't bark):

"No! Stop! Don't hurt him!"

Everyone is looking at us.

The worker aims at One-Eye and shoots. I shriek again. "No!"

But it's not a gun; it's a water gun!

A stream of water hits One-Eye in the face and he backs off the terrier and shakes his head.

"Are you okay?" I ask him.

He half smiles. "Yeah. I'm good. No one will be looking to fight with me for a while, anyway."

The terrier, who has a pretty nasty bite on his neck, yowls and retreats to the corner. After that, the other dogs go right back to whatever they were doing. A few more little fights break out. The puppies don't notice. They don't understand that we have all been abandoned; they just want to play!

As bad as the storm was, I never thought a bunch of dogs could be so ornery. I try not to let anyone see how bad my back legs are shaking, so I walk around the edge of the yard, keeping my head low.

We are herded back inside and I stay close to One-Eye for a little extra insurance. I'm becoming more like him; suspicious of all the other dogs.

When we get back, I collapse, exhausted and oddly relieved to be in the cage again. I lie down, but this time One-Eye doesn't tell me to move.

"Where do you live?" I ask, as I watch him chew a bald patch on his front paw.

"The street."

"You don't have a home?"

He relaxes a little, but every time there's movement in the hall, his ears pick up. He growls when anyone gets near the door of our cage, but not as loudly as before.

"I worked on a car lot for a while."

What's a car lot?

"But one night I ran away."

"Why?"

"I don't like humans. They have too many rules."

He falls into a half-sleep and I stay awake even though I'm very tired. I wonder what he'll do when we all go home. I try to stay awake because I want to listen for George.

One-Eye sits up again and scratches. He had bald patches on his chest and flank, and he's got an oozy cut on his shoulder from the fight in the yard.

"Have you been in a lot of fights?"

He doesn't answer. He looks away.

I've been rude.

"I'm sorry."

I roll over and fall asleep, and I don't wake up until I hear the metal food bowls clanging. When someone sets our bowl down, we both eat. One-Eye still gets more, but he doesn't try to prevent me from having a share.

There's a lot of activity in the hallway. Some of the dogs are being rounded up for transport to another shelter. I watch as the three across from us are leashed up and led away. The dogs are all nervous and wondering aloud where they're going.

A lady opens our cage door and One-Eye growls.

"Oh yeah?" she says to him. "Well, growl all you want—you're leaving, and we're happy to see you go."

I line up right behind him, politely waiting to be leashed.

"No, not you. You're staying here," she says.

I'm shattered. I've known One-Eye for only a day, but somehow we became friends. The lady is looking over some papers when One-Eye murmurs, "That was nice of you last night."

I stare at him.

"The way you stepped up."

I don't want to cry. I stand straight and say, "Good luck."

"You too."

And just like that he's gone, and I'm alone again.

I'm left to cheer myself up. What can I do?

First, I hope.

I hope Mamma and George will find me soon.

But I start to get worried about that when somebody new comes by my cage. She puts a white sign on it. The sign has two black letters.

"Hi, TJ!" she says. "That's your new name!"

New name? I don't need a new name. I have a name. Jimmy.

This lady with the sign seems nice, and she scratches my ears through the bars. But if Mamma and George come, they will ask for Jimmy. And the people here will say, "Sorry. We have no Jimmys."

Somebody opens up our cages. We are taken outdoors

again. No one starts any trouble with me.

Some dogs are talking around me, giving and getting advice on how to get people to notice you and want to take you home. But I've lost my voice and can't join in. I don't want to anyway.

"Jump on the front of the cage!"

"No! They don't like jumpers."

"Bark loud!"

"No, that'll scare 'em!"

Then I see him headed my way. It's the terrier! And he's got two big friends with him.

"Here's the one," he says, and stops right in front of me.

The other dogs slink away.

I sit very still. And quiet. If I'm good, maybe he'll leave me alone.

But the shelter worker comes over and the terrier pretends he was just playing. We're put back into our cages, one at a time.

Chapter 10

Chrissie

Day after day, George and Mamma don't come. Each time I hear footsteps, I think it might be them. But it never is.

Some of the dogs invent ways to get noticed so someone will want them. The mean terrier twirls on his hind legs, as if he's a funny little clown and not a bully. A hound down the row sings a song. It sounds off-key to me, but sure enough, a little girl and her dad are charmed. I hear them leave; they're singing together.

Across from me, there's a dog like Kissy, a fluffy little female. She flirts with everyone who walks by. She yips, and as soon as people turn to look at her, she sits up on her hind legs and waves her paw. Frankly, her act looks fake to me, but it works. In no time, an older lady scoops her up. I watch them leave and feel sad all over again. I can't sing and I'm clumsy, so forget dancing.

But I catch on. Maybe, just maybe, Mamma and George aren't coming after all. And if I want another home, I need to stand out. I'm not big and powerful and I'm not small and adorable. I'm medium. I have no talent and I don't know any fancy tricks. As a matter of fact, I don't know any simple tricks either. My coat isn't spotted, striped, or brindle. I'm the color of plain vanilla ice cream. I'm an ordinary dog with a pleasant personality. But I'm a good boy. That's what Mamma and George always say. "You're a good boy, Jimmy."

Hold on a second! Maybe that's it: I have very nice manners. I don't jump on people, or bother them by barking or howling. I *never* beg for food or attention. There have to be folks who'll want a friendly, well-mannered dog. When people come, I'll sit quietly and politely. I'll wag my tail because everybody likes a happy dog. I get it. I'm ready now.

I think someone's coming. Look sharp. Good posture. Head high. Smile!

Squish. Squish.

I can hear the plop of sneakers on the wet cement floor. A pretty girl is walking between the rows of cages.

Squish. Squish. Here she comes. This is my chance.

I cock my head. I perk up my ears. She keeps walking right past me and doesn't even glance in my direction.

I lie down in my cage to have a little cry. I feel like a baby. But then I realize that I can't fold up at every little disappointment. I like this girl. She has a kind face. If she comes this way again, I'm going to get her to pay some attention to me.

I hear the *squish squish* coming back my way. Showtime! I sit up nice and straight, but I can't seem to tuck my back leg in. It's flopping off to the side. *Wake up, Jimmy. Sit like a grown-up.* Never mind. She's here. I stare straight into her eyes and wag happily. I'm smiling so hard, half my upper lip sticks to my gums. Rats. My smile is crooked and I can't do a thing about it.

She walks by, and this time she stops. I stand up and wag so hard my butt bangs into the side of the cage. That makes her smile. Maybe being clumsy isn't so terrible. Could it get me a home?

"Well, you're a sweet ol' boy," she says.

Yes! That's exactly what I am! Not a big-time dancing or singing star, but a sweet ol' boy. The girl is friendly and gentle. She opens up my cage and loops a long leather cord around my neck. I'm so excited that I trip over it as we're walking down the hallway. One of the dogs snickers, but I hold my head high.

We go to the yard and sit on the grass together. It's still soggy, but the sun is shining. I rest my paws on her shoulders.

"Oh, you're giving me a hug, little boy. I like hugs!" She hugs me back.

I think it's working. I really think it's working. I'll miss Mamma and George, but I need a home. I can't stay at that shelter forever. I have to hope this girl will like me.

I nuzzle my nose gently under her chin.

Please, please take me home.

"How would you like to leave here and live with a new

52

family?" she asks, giving my ears a little scratch. "See, TJ, I'm here to find you a new family."

I knew it! I knew she was going to take me home!

"I bet you must miss your folks, but I'm going to have to find you some new ones, okay?"

Find me some new ones? What does that mean? Isn't she going to take me home herself? I lick her face, to remind her how cute I am. How I'm a sweet ol' boy.

"I guess that's a yes," she says, laughing.

Her name is Chrissie, and she explains, as she scratches my back—*oh, yes, right there, that feels good!*—that she's a volunteer helping to find us homes. After she's done scratching, she takes out a little notebook and makes some notes.

"How old do we think you are, TJ?"

I'm a puppy, but I'm very mature for my age. And the name's Jimmy.

"I'd guess you're almost a year old."

Yes, that sounds about right.

"And you're a yard dog. I can tell that because you got tangled in your leash."

Is that what you call it? I've never seen one of those before.

"And you're very people-friendly."

Yes, I most certainly am.

"Do you think you'd like a family with other dogs and cats?"

I have to think about this. If I tell the truth (no, I don't like cats and I can do without puppies and I don't care for yappy dogs), then will I hurt my chances of getting a new home? Or if I lie and say, "I love all animals," will I be stuck with a house full of hissing cats and yappers?

I decide to snuggle up very close to Chrissie and hope for the best.

"Hmm. I think you should be with people who'll pay you a lot of attention."

Yes! A lot of attention! Exactly right!

"Well, look at you waggin' your heart out! I'll put down 'No other animals.'"

You're a genius.

"Okay then, TJ, I'd better get to work finding you a home."

After making all her notes, Chrissie takes me back to my cage. There's a new dog in my cage, a big floppy sheepdog. She's nice enough, but I don't feel like talking to her. I miss Mamma and George. I even miss Chrissie, and I only just met her. I really thought she was going to take me home.

I curl up in my cage and think about my new home. But then I fall asleep and dream about my old one. My tummy hurts more and more. I can't understand how my nice life could go so wrong.

Then I realize that if the man in the yellow raincoat hadn't come along, I'd be drowned by now. Or bobcat food. And if Chrissie wasn't here to help me out, I'd be stuck watching *other* dogs leave with new parents.

So stop complaining and buck up, mister! As Mamma used to say, "Count your blessings."

It takes a couple of days, but finally, Chrissie comes for

me. My tummy's really sore now. I never knew being homesick could hurt so bad! I even left half of my food in my bowl this morning, and that's never happened before.

Still, I put a smile on my face and a wag in my tail as soon as Chrissie appears. I don't want her to change her mind.

"How's my sweet ol' boy?"

Fine, thanks. (Except for my stomachache, but why mention it?)

She opens my cage and carries me out into the bright sunlight. She opens the back door of her little car and I climb in.

"We have to get you to the vet for a checkup, TJ."

Huh? What about the new home you promised?

"You have to be healthy before you can start your journey," Chrissie says.

Journey? I'm not staying in Lake Charles?

I'm not happy to hear this news. (Honestly, I'm trying my best.) If Chrissie can't keep me herself, and she can't take me back to Mamma and George, why can't she find me a place nearby? My tummy is so sore that I have to lie on my side all the way to the vet's office.

When we walk in, I freeze. It's the smell. I can smell the fear of all the other animals who have been here before me. Chrissie lifts me onto a cold steel table and I try to jump off.

Never mind. Take me back to the shelter!

"Calm down. Nothing bad is going to happen," Chrissie whispers.

But that's not true. I've been to these places before. There's plenty of bad, even if you don't count the cold, slippery table and the terrifying smells. There are the shots!

But Chrissie keeps petting my head and holding me, and I don't try to run away. I'm still trying hard to show her my good manners. The doctor comes in. He's wearing a white coat. He smells of soap and something that stings my nose.

He listens to my heart and presses on my tummy.

Ouch!

He murmurs something to Chrissie. She kisses the top of my head.

"I'm sorry, little boy, but you'll have to stay here for a few days because you're sick."

I *know* I'm sick—I'm homesick! But why do I have to stay here? Can't I go to your house?

Chrissie rubs my sore tummy very softly and sings a little tune in my ear. I put my face close to hers and sniff her hair.

"That tickles," she says with a smile. She gives me a good-bye pat.

No! Don't go!

"You be patient, TJ. And I'll be back as soon as you're feeling better."

And now she's walking away. Her comforting smell lingers, and then the door shuts behind her, and she's gone.

Gone!

Road Trip

Not another cage! But here it is and here I am in it. My tummy hurts and I'm too sad about Chrissie leaving to put up any kind of a fight. Besides, I'm trying to be sweet and good so I can move to a new home.

A nurse gives me something really tasty to eat. I gulp it down, even though I didn't feel like eating before. Then she tells me to relax and rest and says I'll feel better when the medicine starts working.

Being stuck in here is lonely. Having nothing better to do, I chew my paws and whimper. I'm not one of those dogs who cries a lot, but there are times when it just feels good to let go of sad feelings. After a few whimpers, I feel a tiny bit better. Then I fall asleep for heaven knows how long.

An amazing thing happens next: I wake up and the tummy ache's almost gone. I'm better! Not great, like I felt on Sundays, but not terrible, like I've been feeling since I got to the shelter. Who knew they made a medicine for being homesick?

I wait and wait. I'm getting to be pretty good at waiting. People walk past my door and they bring me water, and then they bring me more medicine and a little food, and later on more food. I sleep some more. I can't tell if it's night or day. The lights are on in here all the time. I just sleep when I get sleepy, and it seems like I'm sleepy a lot of the time.

Sometimes I dream about Mamma and George, and my yard, and my holes, and my bone that I left there. Once I dream about the storm, and I wake up crying. A nurse comes and pets my head.

Once I dream about Chrissie.

And when I wake up, she's come back, just like she promised. She's here to pick me up!

They let me out of my cage. Chrissie kneels down and I jump right into her arms.

"Guess what, TJ? I've found you a real nice family and we're going to meet them soon! I'll take you myself."

A real nice family? I wag, but I'm pretending. I guess I should be relieved, but I'm not.

First, I thought Mamma and George were sure to come for me. Then I thought Chrissie would take me herself. Now there's this other family somewhere. It's hard to feel excited. I don't know what this new family will be like.

Chrissie gives me a big kiss.

"You'll be happy again, little boy."

No, I won't.

"You will, I promise."

There she goes, reading my mind again.

Okay, I tell myself. *You have to grow up. And if you can't really grow up, then for Pete's sake, just pretend.* But it's no use. I start to cry and can't stop. Chrissie understands and gives me a big cuddle. She takes her time stroking my back slowly and gently. She scratches behind my ears.

"Come on! We're going to have big fun."

My idea of big fun is Sunday supper and a nap. I think Chrissie has different ideas. She puts one of those leash things on my collar and walks me out of the building. Even though I'm feeling better, I hope I never have to come back.

We get into her car and I look out the back window. Maybe I'll hear George's truck. He'll jump out just before we leave and Mamma will be right behind him calling my name and waving a pork chop.

I hear Mamma. "Woohoo, Jimmy! Come help me hang the wash."

And George. "You have a good day now, you hear?"

I even hear Kissy. "It's raining. Let me in!"

That's how it should be. But I guess it's not going to be that way ever again.

We pull out of the parking lot and onto a big noisy road. I press my nose against the window. I whimper.

"I know just how to cheer you up, little boy."

Not a chance.

Chrissie pops in a CD and sings along. She knows all the words and bops her head back and forth in time to the music.

You ain't nothing but a hound dog . . .

Hmm . . . A song about a dog!

You ain't never caught a rabbit and you ain't no friend of mine!

I'm not completely cheered up yet.

We keep driving and driving. Chrissie pulls the car up a ramp and onto a wide road with lots of other cars zipping by fast. There's nothing much to do but go to sleep.

I sleep, and when I wake up I still think I'm back on the porch. Or in the storm. Or in a cage. Then I realize I'm in Chrissie's car on the way to a new family. I stretch and poke my head over the front seat. Chrissie looks straight ahead, but reaches back and gives my head a pat.

"Your new people are from New York City," she says. She peeks into the little car mirror and winks at me. "They talk a little different, but you'll get the hang of them."

Each time we stop, I look around for my new people, but the stops are just little breaks from driving. Chrissie takes me for walks so we can both stretch our legs.

When it starts to get dark, she pulls off the road and we get out of the car at a big building with lots of rooms. In our room she puts out a bowl of water and some food for me, but I'm too nervous to eat.

"Life is a big adventure, little boy," she tells me. "And you have to go with the flow."

She lets me curl up on the bed next to her as she watches TV. I see pictures of the storm, of the water swirling around houses, of people stuck on roofs just like I was. I stick my head down into the blankets and shut my eyes. I don't want to think about the storm. I don't want to think about any of it.

But in the morning I remember what Chrissie said—*go with the flow*. I'm not sure what she meant. But I think she meant not to stick my head in the blankets and stay that way.

So today I put my head out the car window and take in the sights and smells. I see another dog in the backseat of a convertible: a golden retriever, a cousin. I give her a big smile as we roll by. She smiles back. Rats. I wish we could stop and sniff around.

Chrissie notices.

"You'll make lots of friends in New York City," she assures me.

Chrissie sings and drives, and I look out the window, and we keep going for another couple of days. Then, just as I feel like I'm getting the hang of this "go with the flow" business, Chrissie pulls the car off the highway. She takes us to another motel and we find our room. I'm ready to cuddle up with Chrissie in the bed and watch another movie, but it turns out that something else is going on.

"Look, little boy!" Chrissie calls out. She's peering out the window. "Over there! That's your new mom and dad getting out of their car. They've come for you!"

And a weird thing is happening: I'm too scared to move.

I just huddle down on the carpet and start to shiver.

Why? After all, I'm rescued and I'm going to live with my brand-new family.

But I remember what Chrissie said: They talk a little different, but *I'll get the hang of them.* What if I don't? What if I can't understand the way they talk? What if they *don't like me?*

My life in Lake Charles was so simple. I knew everything I needed to know. Mamma and George loved me and I loved them.

My *new* parents have just come through the door of our motel room. They are sitting on the floor and taking turns patting my head and rubbing my back.

"Look how sweet he is," the new mom says.

"He's kind of puny," the new dad says.

I look at Chrissie and I look at the mom and dad and I feel very, very sad. I slide over to her and bury my head in her lap. Chrissie and I have become good friends. Now she's going to leave me with these strangers. I don't want to go.

The mom reaches into a bag and gives me a toy duck. I have no idea what to do with it. To be polite, I sniff it, then look away. She puts it back in her bag. Chrissie's crying. Can't she just take me back to her house? I can tell she's sad to be leaving me behind.

The new dad is looking out the motel window. He glances at his watch.

"Let's go or we'll hit traffic," he says to the new mom.

I know this whole thing is a bad idea. I want to stay with Chrissie, and the new people can get a shelter dog the dad will like better. A less "puny" dog. Whatever that means.

I wiggle under the bed. Leave without me, okay?

Chrissie and the new mom reach under and try to coax me out. I don't let them. Since I've left my yard, I've ended up somewhere I didn't really want to be—the water, a roof, the shelter. It doesn't seem to me like this new home with my new parents is going to be any better.

Finally the dad says, "Okay. Time to go. Give him a yummy or something to get him out of there."

Humph. I'm not budging.

Wait. What's that smell? Is that chicken?

My legs still want to stay under the bed, but my nose seems to take over. Before I know it, I'm out and gulping down something tasty from my new mom's hand.

The mom snaps a leash to my collar. She and Chrissie are hugging each other good-bye. The dad is jiggling his leg and twirling his car keys. He looks about as happy as I feel.

I'm still hoping Chrissie will change her mind, so I do something I *never* do because it's rude: I jump up on Chrissie and rest my paws on her hips. I know she'll understand why.

She kneels beside me, puts her arms around my neck, and whispers, "Time to start your new life, little boy. Go on now. And don't forget to mind your manners."

And just like that, my new life begins.

Chapter 12

The New People

When we get into the car, my new mom and dad both get in the front seat. And the dad starts the car. He pulls out of the parking lot like he's in a hurry.

I stand on the backseat looking for Chrissie and crying. The new mom catches on pretty quickly.

"I think I'll sit in the back with him," she tells the dad.

The dad stops the car and sighs. I don't think he's very happy about the seating arrangement. The mom holds me close, and it feels good. She picks up my earflap and gently whispers, "I know you're scared, but it'll be fine."

I wouldn't exactly call it "fine."

Nobody says much, and the trip isn't big fun like it had been with Chrissie. The dad turns on the radio and punches the buttons until he finds the traffic report. All the cars around us are stopped and there is a lot of honking.

"Oh, great. An accident." He's really mad now. "We won't be home until late." He bangs the steering wheel and I start shaking, but I don't make a peep. I know I can't bark, and what's the use of crying?

"You're scaring the dog," the mom says nervously.

This is not looking like my dream family.

"What a dumb idea," the dad grumbles. "There are so many homeless dogs in New York and you had to pick *this* one."

I don't move. I'm frozen right there in the backseat. If I move, something awful might happen. The dad might open the car door and toss me right out. Then what will I do?

The mom lifts my ear and whispers, "Don't worry, pup. I have it under control."

Then she says, "Larry, if you don't like him, we can find him another home."

What? Is this what she means by having it under control?

"Oh please, Jane, you're already in love with him," Larry grumbles over his shoulder. The cars around us start to move and he begins driving again.

"See?" the mom whispers in my ear.

And I learn three new things in that moment: First, Dad's name is Larry. Second: Mom's name is Jane. And third, Jane already loves me.

But Larry doesn't.

"Wait till you meet Brian," Jane announces as Larry pulls up in front of a house in the middle of the busiest street I've ever seen. Is it safe to get out? Cars everywhere, people hurrying along in every direction, so much noise! Honking, shouting, rumbling. The street shakes from the weight of the traffic. I poke my head between the seat and Jane's rear end and decide to stay right there. It's cozy here in the backseat and I could get used to it.

"You'll see. You'll be a city dog in no time," Jane whispers. *I'll never be a city dog.*

"Dare to be brave, sweet pea," she adds, twisting around to kiss the top of my head. I peek up at her and catch sight of a boy, about eleven or twelve years old, at the top of the stoop. He's pointing at the car and waving.

"There's Brian, and he's waiting to meet you!"

When Jane opens the back door, Brian comes flying down the steps, giving a holler that would give the mightiest of dogs a migraine.

He dives into the backseat and winds his long skinny arms around my neck and presses the tip of my ear between his lips and hums. It doesn't hurt, but it feels a little strange. He holds me like that until Jane says, "Honey, we need to unload the car. Take the leash and walk him a little."

"Listen, buddy," Brian whispers when he finally lets go of my ear. "We're going to be best friends. I'll teach you everything you need to know." Then he takes the leash and gives it a tug. Ouch. Why do I have to be tied up like this?

"Brian, be careful. He's been sick, and we all have to treat him gently."

"Okay, Mom."

With Brian tugging, I climb out of the car into an explosion of smells and noise. The heat from the pavement burns my paw pads, and the sounds of engines and sirens make me shudder. A yellow car screeches and swerves, nearly hitting a woman whose arm is raised. I pull back.

"Relax," Brian says. "It's just a woman hailing a cab. Welcome to New York City."

Hailing a what? Looked like an almost-accident to me.

So this was New York City. And Chrissie thought I'd *get used to it*? These are the people she thought I'd *get the hang of*? I can hardly understand what they're saying!

The street is like nothing I've ever seen or smelled. There must be a million dogs who have walked here. In Lake Charles, the only street I could see was outside our house, and hardly any dogs walked on it. Most of us were tied up in the yard or kept behind a fence.

Whoa. The smells here are *wonderful*.

"So here's the deal," Brian says as I begin to take in all the scents. "Are you listening?"

No. I'm sniffing, and I can't really give you my attention right now.

"So here's the deal," he repeats. "First rule is you have to be a Yankee fan."

Wow, there are wire cans on the street and they're full of food. There's a hot dog in this one. *Ooh. Lemme at it!*

"Hey! Get away from the garbage."

Garbage? Are you kidding? This is a banquet hall. I can smell the hot dog from here.

"I know you're from New Orleans, which means you're probably a what? A Braves fan? But you'll have to switch to the Yankees. They're your home team now."

It's behind a newspaper. But it's trapped in the can. I bet if I jump I can knock it over.

"Quit pulling. There's no way you're getting in the garbage. We're going home."

What's the rush? There are leftovers, soda spills, crumbs, and at least a thousand different dog poop and pee smells. I'm dizzy from all the choices.

"Let's go," Brian says, and he pulls the leash so hard I have no choice but to follow. *Phooey.*

Larry's gone off to park the car, and Jane is waiting in front of the house. We go up the stairs, and another lady meets us at the front door.

"This is Val," Brian says. "She stays with me when my parents are away." He gives me a stern look. "But she's *not* a babysitter because I'm way too old for that. Got it?"

"Hi, doggie," Val says and gives me a pat. "Does he have a name yet?"

Yes, my name is Jimmy.

"No. I'm going to name him. Mom and Dad said I could."

He's going to decide? Why? Is he the boss? He's a kid who puts dog ears in his mouth. What are these people thinking?

Maybe I *would* be better off with another family. Jane's not bad, but Larry is a grump and the kid's very strange.

Chrissie, what have you done to me?

Chapter 13

So Long, Jimmy

I'm thirsty from the trip, and as soon as we go into the kitchen I find my water and food bowls. I slurp up the water. There's kibble there, too, but it doesn't look that good compared to the hot dog I had my eye on outside. I don't like how the kibble smells, and if something doesn't smell good, you shouldn't eat it.

Larry comes inside and hangs up his coat. "Brian," I hear him say. "What do you think?"

"He's cool, Pop."

"What does he look like to you?"

We gather in the living room. Larry's in a better mood. He's not talking about how *puny* I am or what a dumb idea it was to get me. They all sit in silence for a while and study my face.

What's going on, guys?

70

"I think we should call him Newman," Jane says thoughtfully.

"Nope," Larry says right away. "He doesn't look like a Newman."

"Ew, Newman. That sucks," Brian brays.

Jane and Larry glare at him.

"Well, it does. It's like a teacher's name."

Larry shakes his finger at Brian. "Look. I'm tired and not in the mood for your smart mouth."

"Could we not stress, please?" Jane begs. "I made a list of possible names." She runs up the stairs and comes right back with a pad.

"Stop me when you like one," she says a little breathlessly. "Milton, Murray."

"Murray? Are you kidding?" Brian yells. "You name an old bald guy Murray."

"Harry, Ben, Logan, Bubba, Yoda, Steve, Pinsky . . ."

"Pinsky?" Larry sneers.

Larry's right about this one. Imagine introducing myself as *Pinsky* to a new friend.

"Scratch Pinsky," Brian orders.

"Okay," Jane mutters. "No need to get hostile about it."

I trot over to sit beside Jane, since she has the list. There's a rug in the living room, but it doesn't cover the whole floor. There's a little strip of polished wood near Jane that's slippery. My front paw gets away from me. *Whoops!* The corner of the rug bunches up and I go flying into the side of the coffee table.

Larry and Brian burst out laughing. Jane kneels down to see if I'm okay. I'm fine. But I feel like a major *clod*. No one would ever believe I made my way between two roofs above a flood! I just look like a clumsy little puppy. A useless, *puny,* clumsy little puppy.

Larry looks at Brian and says, "Why don't we name him Thud?"

"That's so mean, Dad!" Brian says, but he's still laughing.

Jane scowls and goes on with her list. "Herbie, Kramer, Roger—"

Larry cuts in. "I think Thud works. He's a klutz. He flops over if you look at him."

Jane gives Larry a dirty look.

"It's a lame name," Brian says, getting back to business.

"We don't have to name him tonight," Larry says restlessly.

Yes! If we wait, maybe someone will come up with Jimmy.

"I don't know." Jane shrugs.

Suddenly everybody's getting grouchy.

"Wait!" Brian says. "I think I got it."

"Well, get on with it then," Larry snaps.

"Oh, relax," Jane snaps right back. She isn't one bit afraid of Larry! I wish I could be brave like her.

"Hooper!" Brian shouts.

There's a little pause. Then Jane beams. "Yeah! Hooper. I like it."

"I like Thud," Larry says glumly.

But Brian's made up his mind. He grins at me. "Come here, Hooper!"

I stay put. Maybe if I wait, they'll keep looking for another name. How about it, Jane? Anything left on your list?

On the other hand, they might come up with something worse than Pinsky. (Is that possible?)

Brian calls me again. "Here, Hooper!"

Oh, all right. You can call me Hooper if you want, but I'll always be Jimmy.

I walk over to Brian's side. Slowly and carefully. I don't want to slip again.

"C'mon, Hooper, I wanna show you the most important room in the house," Brian calls happily as he runs up the stairs two at a time.

His room is the closest thing to dog dreamland I could possibly imagine. There are piles of deliciously smelly clothes all over the floor and on the bed. I don't know what to roll in first. And the smells! Sweat, poop, pizza. Every smell a dog needs in life. And best of all, the odor of another dog. I sniff a basket of stuff in the corner, where the smell is strongest.

"Those are Hammer's toys." Brian sounds sad for the first time since I got there. "But they're yours now. And I'm sure you'll get a lot of new ones." Brain empties the basket onto the floor, scattering more delicious smells for me to investigate. But the things that roll out are strange. Nothing to do with dogs, as far as I can tell.

73

"See? Here." Brian tosses a ball in my direction. I watch it whiz by my head.

"You're supposed to catch it!"

I am? Why?

"Never mind. We'll play ball later."

Sure. Later. Right now I'm a lot more interested in exploring the smells all around me.

I plop down in the middle of a big pile of clothes and roll. *This is wonderful!* I rub the scent all over my back.

"Why do dogs roll in stuff?" Brian asks, watching me.

That's easy. It's so other dogs will think we smell cool.

"Stay where you are, Hooper!" Brian says eagerly. "I want Dan to see you like that. Dan's my best friend. He lives across the street, so you'll be seeing him a lot."

Brian grabs a phone from under a pile of clothes, presses a button, and holds it up to his ear. "Hey, Dan," he says. "You gotta come over and see the new dog. He's in my room. He's rolling around in my clothes."

There's a pause.

"Oh, yeah, okay. Can you come over tomorrow?"

Another pause.

"Yeah. See ya." Brian tosses the phone down. "He can't come tonight," Brian reports to me. "His mom is making him study for the history test he's going to fail."

"Brian," Larry shouts up the stairs. "Is Thud with you?"

"Yeah, Pops, I got *Hooper* up here."

"Has he broken anything yet?"

74

Why does Larry dislike me? I stop rolling, drop my head, and sigh. Brian sits on the floor next to me and pets my head. I think he understands.

"Listen," he tells me. "He misses our old dog, Hammer, and I have a feeling it's going to take a while for him to get used to you."

I look over at the toys. Hammer's toys.

"They were really big buddies. They played ball every day. Dad hasn't been the same since Hammer died. But I know he's going to love you. We just have to teach him how."

I think about how much Mamma and George loved me and I get even sadder. Nobody had to teach them to love me—they just did.

Jane yells from downstairs. "Bri, I'm going to take Hooper for a quick walk and then I'll keep him in our room overnight."

"But *Mom*—"

"He'll stay in your room when he gets used to it here. I want to keep an eye on him for a few nights."

Brian gives me a hug and lips my ear again.

"Hooper! Let's go!" Jane calls.

I gallop down the stairs, remembering the hot dog around the corner.

Jane doesn't take me past the hot dog on this walk, but there are lots and lots of other good smells. She doesn't let me sniff long enough, though. Every few feet she tugs me along.

The amazing thing is all the dogs I can smell. There must be hundreds of them! I can smell males and females, big and little, healthy and sick. I can smell the ones who just ate kibble this morning and the ones who got delicious scraps—scrambled eggs, bits of sausage, milky bowls of soggy cereal. Yum!

I wonder what kind of a dog Hammer was. Was he a good ol' boy, like me? If Larry liked him, he probably wasn't much like me. Was he tough and strong, like One-Eye? I don't think I can be like that. I don't think I can be any kind of dog that Larry's going to like.

I'm still thinking about this when we get back to the house. Jane opens the front door and leads me upstairs and into her room.

It doesn't smell as good as Brian's room, but it has a huge, soft bed with squishy pillows, fancy blankets, and a fluffy quilt. Hey! This just might be better than sleeping out in the yard or under the porch! Maybe there are *some* things about this new home that could be okay.

Here's something important to know about dogs: We are territorial. That means that we find out how much space belongs to us and we keep an eye on it. We don't want some-body else's dog staking out our bowls, bones, and other spaces we have made our own. These are *ours*.

I begin to figure out how I can make a hunk of that big bed *my* territory.

Larry has stretched out on the left side to watch television. Jane disappears into the bathroom to take a shower. I figure I've got my best shot at the bed when she comes back.

I lie down on the floor and wait quietly and patiently until she returns. I'm minding my manners just like Chrissie told me to.

"Isn't Hooper adorable?" Jane smiles as she opens the door and sees me half snoozing.

"He needs a bath," Larry replies, still staring at the television.

I peek at Jane to see how she'll respond.

"I'll give him a bath tomorrow."

I wonder what a bath is.

Jane climbs into bed on the right side, which leaves me a pretty good slice of space in the middle. As soon as she tucks herself in, I make my move. I scramble between them somewhere at knee level, knowing if I get too close to Larry's face I'll get booted right back to the floor.

"Off the bed!" he orders, but Jane comes right to the rescue.

"He's so scared. Let him stay. Just for tonight."

Larry grumbles and rolls over. "I can see where this is going," he says into his pillow.

So can I, I think to myself happily as I fall into a deep, lovely sleep.

Chapter 14

Day One

Sometime after it's dark, I wake up when Larry angrily pulls a blanket out from under me, grabs his pillow, and stomps off into the night. I'm afraid for a moment or two, but once he's gone, I've got quite a lot of new space to myself. I go back to sleep, snuggled next to Jane. She's nice and warm.

When Jane stirs in the morning, I wriggle my way toward her and she smiles. This looks like a chance for a belly rub, so I flip over and she gets right to work. It seems like this is the beginning of a better day.

It isn't.

Things start to go wrong when we get downstairs and find Larry sleeping on the sofa. He eyes me angrily and mumbles, "That dog kept me up all night. He snores."

"So do you," Jane says.

"It's *my house.*"

Jane sighs and goes into the kitchen to make breakfast. The silence is shattered when Brian bolts down the stairs and bellows, *"Hooper!"*

"Quiet, Brian," Larry says hoarsely. "I barely got any sleep last night because of that dog." Jane and Brian look down at their feet. I look down at my paws.

"Don't get too chummy with him," Larry goes on. "Because we may not keep him."

"What?" Brian shrieks.

May not keep him? I can't believe it.

I mean, I didn't really want to come here. I wanted to go back to Mamma and George's, or stay with Chrissie. But I *am* here now. And I'm starting to find some good things about it. Brian's lovely smelly room. That big soft bed. All the fabulous smells outside.

If Larry decides they're not going to keep me, what will I do? Go to another shelter? Or just live on the streets?

Larry lumbers back up the stairs to bed, and Brian plops on the floor beside me and puts my ear in his mouth.

"Bri, don't do that. It's disgusting. What do you want for breakfast?"

"I'm not eating until Dad changes his mind."

Jane sighs and puts out another bowl of hard, dry kibble, which I don't touch. Nobody eats anything. Jane clears the dishes out of the dishwasher and Brian and I lie on the floor. He twirls his bathrobe tie and stares at the ceiling.

"Mom, why is Dad doing this?"

"Well, you know how Dad hates new situations."

"It's not a new situation. We've had a dog before."

"I know. But let's give him a chance to get used to Hooper. Be patient. Dad will come around."

"What if he doesn't?"

Yeah, Jane. What if he doesn't?

Jane doesn't answer.

Brian lowers his voice so only I can hear him. "Listen, Hooper," he whispers in my ear. "We have to change Dad's mind."

You're dreaming. There's no way he's ever going to like me.

"You have to be more of a jock."

What's a jock?

Brian is thinking very hard, and he twirls his bathrobe tie faster.

"'Cause didn't you have to swim in that storm?"

I wouldn't call it swimming, exactly. More like hopelessly paddling.

"And you can run fast, right?"

No.

"I mean you must be very brave!"

Me, brave? Ha!

Well, on second thought, I didn't drown. And I got away from that bobcat. And I did jump on rafts and roofs.

Maybe just a little brave.

"And you got yourself rescued, so you must be pretty smart."

I think about this, too. Actually, I did convince Chrissie

to rescue me. There were so many dogs at the shelter, but she picked me.

"So, Hooper, you can do things other dogs can't. You're pretty cool."

Brian stares at me, nodding.

Really?

Me?

You mean it?

Brian's nodding like he understands what I'm thinking.

"You're one great dog, all right," he says with determination. "Our new project is to get Dad to notice. Come on up to my room."

Once we get up there, Brian turns on the TV. He calls to Larry, who's walking by in the hall. "Come and watch the game!"

Larry looks in, sees me flopping into a pile of Brian's clothes, rolls his eyes a little, but comes inside. They watch for a while. I used to watch the ballgames with George, so this feels like home to me.

A new home? Could it really be? Unless Larry decides I can't stay.

Then some loud commercials come on. Larry takes his eyes away from the TV, looks at me, and says, "Let's see if this dog of yours can catch a tennis ball."

This dog of yours, I notice. Not *this dog of ours*.

Brian grabs one of Hammer's balls out of the basket.

"Hey!" Larry says. "That's—"

He stops talking. Brian stops moving. He just sits really still with the tennis ball in his hand.

"Nothing," Larry mutters after a long moment. "Just throw the thing."

Brian doesn't throw it. He just reaches over and gives it to me. I take it in my mouth. It's fuzzy. I plop down beside Brian and chew on it for a while.

"Wanna play catch, Hooper?" Brian asks meekly.

Catch?

Brian wrestles the ball from my mouth. "Okay, catch!" And he throws the ball in the air right over my head.

The ball bounces down right in front of my nose. I look at it.

What are they expecting me to do?

I have no idea, so I roll over on my back.

Larry looks at me. "You don't want to play catch?" He picks up the ball and tosses it again. Right at my mouth.

Yikes! I duck and slide under the bed.

"I can't believe this dog is afraid of a tennis ball," Larry snorts.

My heart sinks.

"Hey, guys! What's going on?" Jane asks as she walks in with a tray of very delicious-smelling treats. I come out from under the bed to investigate.

"Thud's afraid of a tennis ball."

"Give him a chance to adjust," Jane protests. "What's the score?"

"Two all."

Whatcha got on that tray, Jane?

"When Dan gets here, we're going to teach Hooper to catch," Brian says firmly.

Fine. What's on the tray?

"Good luck," Larry says, not bothering to look away from the television. "Base hit!"

Brian isn't fazed.

"Pop, you'll eat your words in a week or so."

A week? Try never.

They watch the Yankee game and I watch them eat thick turkey sandwiches and chips. Brian tears off a piece of turkey for me.

"Don't tell," he whispers in my ear.

I know how to keep a secret.

"Hey, I saw that," Larry says. "He gets dog food. Not our food. Understand?"

But each time Brian takes a bite, he looks around and sneaks a little bite for me. Larry is too busy watching the game to notice.

"I have work to do," Larry announces once the game is over. "Bet you twenty bucks you'll never teach that sad excuse for a dog to catch," he adds on his way out.

"You're on, Dad," Brian calls after him. "But we need a little time." He scratches my ears and says in a nice big voice (which I hope Larry hears), "Don't worry, dude. We'll show my grouchy old man."

Brian turns on some kind of movie. It's still on when Dan comes in wearing sunglasses, Yankee cap, and Yankee shirt. Brian grabs a cap and puts it on, too.

"Hooper, this is my lucky hat. When I wear it to games, the Yankees win. So I'm going to wear it to our ball practices. Then we'll definitely win that bet!"

Dan and Brian set up a pile of fuzzy balls. Dan is pitching and Brian is coaching.

"Okay, listen up, Hooper, you have to keep your eye on the ball." I look up in confusion, and he seems to get that I have no idea what he means. "Look at the ball," he explains. "Don't stop watching it, no matter what."

Oh, okay. Looking at a ball is something I can do.

Dan takes a tennis ball from the pile. "Now watch," he commands.

So I watch as Dan gently tosses the ball. I watch it bounce right in front of me.

"No, no, Hooper. You're not supposed to watch it drop; you're supposed to catch it. Now let's try again."

What? You told me to watch it!

This time Dan tosses the ball up in the air, and I watch it hit me in the nose.

Ouch!

"He's kind of a klutz," Dan says, watching me.

"He just needs practice," Brian insists. "Ready?"

No.

"Here we go." Dan tosses the ball in the air, and before it

can hit me in the nose again, I roll over on my back.

"You don't want to learn, do you?" Brian sighs.

No kidding.

"How about just chewing on the tennis ball for now?" He offers it to me.

Now you're talking.

I love the fuzzy coating and the springy rubber underneath. It feels good to bite down on it. *This is fun! Why didn't you just hand it to me in the first place?*

"I think we're going too fast for him," Dan said gently.

"I've got twenty bucks on him," Brian replied. "He has to learn to catch."

"What if he can't?"

"*He can.* He just doesn't want to."

"Brian, you have to ease up. He's not into sports."

"My dad will never like him." Brian sounds really sad.

"He didn't like me in the beginning either," Dan points out. "Now he doesn't mind me."

"Yeah . . . that's true."

Brian looks at me.

"I'm sorry," he says.

I wiggle over to him and keep chewing away on the tennis ball. If learning to catch it will make Larry like me, I guess I can try. But for right now the chewing feels much too good to stop.

85

Chapter 15

The Bath

After my failure at catching, I need to doze off and dream about something happy. I'm just about to slip into a nice sleep when Jane comes in the door. "Bath time!" she says cheerfully. "I've got the water running."

Oh, no. Water? Put it in a bowl and I'll drink it. Otherwise, keep it away from me. Just the sound of the word brings back the worst experience of my life.

I shiver when I think back on those hard, cold drops turning into walls of water. Those horrible currents that washed away my happy life with Mamma and George.

I slink down and try to creep along the floor of Brian's room. Maybe if I'm low to the ground Jane won't be able to see me. Yes, that's it. I'll make myself very small. Invisible, even.

No luck. She gently (but firmly) pulls me by the collar to the bathroom.

No way will I get into that tub, especially while the water is still coming out of the tap. The *shoosh*ing noise scares me and I don't like the splashing, either. Those droplets start out nice and sweet and turn into storms. There must be a way out of here!

Jane closes the bathroom door.

I'm doomed.

I spin around and try to dig a tunnel under the door.

Jane can see that I'm shaking. "Don't worry, Hooper. This water won't hurt you," she promises.

Puhleeze. If you'd been in a huge storm, you wouldn't be so darned calm.

She turns off the water and gestures toward the tub.

No way, ma'am.

I make another run for the door but skid on the wet, slippery tile floor and bonk my head. I wiggle and roll over on my back. I go totally limp so she can't pick me up. I whimper. I sneeze, which is not part of the plan; it just happens.

My back legs are shaking, and I droop my head in pitiful helplessness.

Jane sits down on the floor. I can tell she feels guilty. Maybe I'll win her over. I plop down and put my head in her lap.

"I guess we should wait until you're ready." She sighs and opens the door.

Hah!

I tear into Brian's room and slide under his bed. I wiggle into the middle so my tail won't stick out and give me away. I don't make a sound.

87

Then I hear a voice almost as scary as the storm.

"If you can't do it, I will."

Larry stomps down the hall and the floor shakes. (Or maybe that's me.) He reaches under the bed and I slide out of range.

So Larry moves the bed.

Rats. I didn't think of that!

"Come on, Hooper. Let's go," he commands.

This guy does not kid around. He drags me down the hall to the bathroom. Jane is still waiting there.

"Let's get on with it," Larry says. He picks me up.

The tub is about half full and there are bubbles floating on the top. I don't like the smell; it's a girly smell. Something Kissy would like.

As if she's read my thoughts, Jane says, "It's dog shampoo, Hooper. It will make your coat nice and clean and soft."

Who wants to be nice and clean and soft? I want to be *dry*.

As Larry lowers me into the water, I panic.

No! No! I'm going to drown. That hole in the tub is going to suck me under. I can hear it gurgling. Where's that man in the yellow slicker with the door boat?

Help me! I try to bark again, but nothing but a gravelly little sound comes out. So I shriek instead. It sounds like a very loud whimper. *Save me!*

"Oh, for Pete's sake!" Larry scowls. "It's just a bath. Hammer never acted like this!"

"Knock it off, Larry. He's scared to death."

Larry lowers his voice. "Fine. But what's that noise he's making? He sounds like a sick seagull. Can't he even bark?"

My whole body is trembling. *I'm begging you. Take me out of here. I'll do anything!*

The two of them go to work massaging the shampoo into my coat. *Hey! Careful with that! Don't get it in my eyes!*

After they work the shampoo from one end to the other, they turn the tap back on. I shriek even louder. A huge spurt of water comes through the faucet. *That's it! I'm leaving!*

I heave myself out of the tub and dive for the door. No luck. Big Larry is in the way.

So I do the next best thing: I shake as much of the soap and water off as I can. I don't want *one drop* on my coat. I shake from head to tail.

Then I look around. There are bubbles and puddles all over the floor. All over the bathtub. All over Larry.

"Ow. You got soap in my eye," he whines. He spits. "Suds in my mouth too."

How do you like it? I promise you it's nothing compared to being in a real storm. Not fun, huh?

Jane rubs me with a big warm towel, but I've got water in my right ear. I shake my head violently, but I can't get it out. I feel like I've been through another storm.

Enough! Stop drying me and *let me out of the bathroom!*

Finally they do. I slink back down the hall and under Brian's bed.

Even dogs need privacy.

I fall asleep under there, and when I wake up, I need to go out. I can't hear the sound of water running anywhere, so I'm probably safe.

I wiggle out from under the bed and nudge Brian. I figure he'll get it.

"Come watch with me, Hooper. It's a double-header!"

I'm not sure what a double-header is, but it's clear he's not going to move. I trot across the hall, where Jane is at the computer. I stare at her. *Look at me! I need to go out!*

"Larry!" she calls. "Hoop needs to go out and I'm work-ing."

"Brian's legs broken?" Larry shouts back.

"The Sox have two men on, no outs!" Brian yells.

"I knew it. This is why I didn't want another dog. He just got here and I have to do all the work," Larry fumes.

"You never complained about taking Hammer out," Jane says, her eyes still on the computer screen, typing fast.

"This dog," Larry says grimly, "is *not* Hammer."

This is definitely a bad idea. I wonder if Larry will dump me in the woods somewhere. But I have to take a chance; I really need to go out.

I sit politely by the front door until Larry gets there. He hooks the leash on my collar. We head outside and walk down the stoop. Right away I get nervous. I'm not sure if I'm sup-posed to walk in front of Larry or behind him. I hesitate and let him go first, then I rush to catch up. But I get tangled up in the stupid leash and I stumble. Unfortunately, I trip Larry and he stumbles, too. He catches himself from falling by grabbing the handrail.

"Try not to break my neck, okay?"

My legs are shaking. I've done something wrong *again*.

"Oh, stop it." Larry sighs. "Act like a dog."

I've been here *one day* and I'm already a *failure*. I'm a klutz. I can't catch a ball and I hate baths and I can't even walk nicely on a leash.

Just then, Larry waves to the man in front of the house next door. He's walking his dog. Maybe I can have a friend! I could sure use some help.

"Hey, Larry," Larry says almost cheerfully.

Two Larrys? That's confusing.

"Hey! That the new dog?" Other Larry asks.

"Yeah," answers Larry without enthusiasm. Then he looks at Other Larry's dog and smiles.

"How ya doin', Wilbur?"

Wilbur and I look each other over. He's a big, macho dog. There are twigs and bits of leaf and burrs in his coat. My coat still smells like perfume. He's going to hate me.

"So you're new, huh?" he says. He's polite, but a bird on the corner pecking an apple core seems to interest him more.

"Yes, today's my first day."

"How's it goin'?" The bird flies off and he turns to me.

"Well, they almost drowned me in the bathtub." The minute I say it I feel stupid. I don't even know him and I'm complaining like a baby.

"Bummer. So you heading to the run?" Wilbur asks.

"What's a run?" I ask and feel stupid again.

"The dog run in the park. It's where dogs get together and hang out. Run around and stuff."

Larry and Other Larry are talking about a new restaurant that has opened in the neighborhood.

I never used to hang out with other dogs back home. Not even Kissy. Will the dog run be like the shelter? The idea makes me shudder.

"Are the dogs friendly?" I ask a little nervously.

"All except Mel. We left when he showed up. He and me don't get along."

"Who's Mel?"

"You can't miss him."

With that, Wilbur gives a big tug on his leash and Other Larry gets the hint.

"See ya," Wilbur calls over his shoulder as he goes up the steps to his house.

"Yeah. See ya," I say, trying to sound cool like him. Trying to sound like I'm not worried about a dog run full of strangers and one mean one named Mel.

We head off to the park, and I'm extra careful not to trip. The closer we get, the more anxious I become. I wish One-Eye were here. He'd know what to do.

And then I see it.

Holy moly.

Chapter 16

The Run

There, in front of us, is a huge fenced-in area. It's bigger than my whole yard at George and Momma's house, and it's full of dogs. Some are running around in a huge circle like a swarm of mosquitoes after a rain.

Oh boy. And there, at the front of the swarm, is Mel. Wilbur's right; nobody could miss him. Is he really a dog? Look at the size of that head! Tufts of spiky gray-brown hair shoot out in every direction; his paws are crusted with mud and his cold eyes are fixed straight ahead, ready to drill into anyone who gets in his way. Syrupy drool drips from his lips, and his huge tongue, which is hanging out, reminds me of the wash flapping on Mamma's clothesline.

There are dogs of all shapes and sizes. Several Labs, much bigger than me, a panting poodle, four or five mutts, and a Jack Russell terrier who could outrun them all if he had four legs instead of three. None of them get in Mel's way.

Near the gate, there is a beautiful bearded collie who stands alone, taking in the scene but not part of it. Other dogs are watching from the sidelines. A basset hound lounges on a bench with his mom, his ears draped across her lap. A spotted mutt is gasping for breath. Several dogs gather around a giant water bowl to gossip.

"Dude, that's *my* Frisbee!"

"Looks like Mel's in a good mood today."

"Will you get a load of Tina's buzz cut?"

Mel's voice cuts through the chatter. "Look out, Ben!" he booms at a Dalmatian who's in the path of the swarm, chasing a pink rubber ball.

"Sorry, sorry!" Ben squeaks back and quickly scrambles under a nearby bench.

There's *no way* I'm going into this place. I don't know a soul and I don't want to. I sit down and refuse to move when Larry tugs at the leash.

"You scared?" he asks, and rolls his eyes.

What do you think?

"Come on. You'll make some friends."

Humph. I'd like to see you walk into a room full of strangers, Mr. Big Shot.

"Okay. We'll just stand here and watch. Of course, everyone will know you're too chicken to go in."

I remember One-Eye warning me not to look weak. But I am weak. What's the point of going in there and having

94

Mel—and who knows how many other dogs—maul me?

Larry shifts his weight from foot to foot, and I have a feeling he's bored. Come on, Larry. Let's go home. But just then Mel's dad calls him, puts his leash on, and starts to go out the gate. As they're leaving, all the dogs call out.

"See you later, Mel."

"Bye, big guy! Take my ball if you want!"

"That was soooo fun."

I can't believe how they're sucking up. One-Eye would have this character begging for mercy.

Mel and his dad turn and walk in our direction. (Just my luck.) Larry tightens his grip on the leash and pulls me closer. I move off the path, so I won't get in Mel's way. When he passes by, I nod politely. I have always been proud of my manners.

Mel mutters, not even bothering to look at me, "My dog run, Shorty. Got it?"

I tremble as he goes by. I can feel the air as he moves, and it makes me shiver. It's almost as bad as the storm. I squat and pee.

The guy who owns Mel looks over his shoulder. "Nice-looking dog," he calls. "What's her name?"

Larry doesn't answer. We take a shortcut out of the park and go straight home.

"Your dog pees like a girl," Larry calls out as soon as we walk in the door.

Thanks a lot. I flop down and want to hide my head under

my paws. *All* puppies pee like that! I know older male dogs lift their legs, but I just haven't learned how yet. He doesn't have to make such a big deal of it!

Jane's putting out my dinner. She frowns.

"Don't be mean. And give me a hand moving the table for tomorrow," she orders. He hustles right over.

I have to learn how she bosses him around and gets away with it. The idea of food perks me up. I go over and stick my nose into the bowl. More dry kibble.

"What's tomorrow?" Larry asks as he pushes the table into a new place.

"You know. Sunday. We're having a welcome party for Hooper!"

Whoa. I almost stop eating. A party? For me?

"What are we having?" Larry asks.

"Salmon."

Salmon? Salmon's my favorite! Well, except for roast beef.

"And I ordered a big roast beef bone for Hooper."

Oh, joy!

Jane bends over and scratches my back.

"You're going to meet our friends tomorrow!" she tells me. "And Wilbur is coming!"

Oh, good!

"You're both gonna have *fun*," she adds.

I'm curious about what she means by fun. And I'm *really* excited about the menu.

Chapter 17

My Party

I'm still excited the next day, when the doorbell rings. It's Other Larry, his wife, Ann, and Wilbur. Much to Ann's horror, Wilbur makes himself at home by crashing into the house, jumping up on the kitchen counter, and demolishing a block of Swiss cheese. Ann is furious at him, but he doesn't look a bit sorry. What guts! New Yorkers do things that southerners would never do. Wilbur smacks his lips happily, burps, and stretches out in the middle of the living room.

"Good cheese," he tells me before dozing off.

Jane's best friend, Deborah, and her daughter, Rosie, arrive next with two shopping bags for me! The first bag holds a bright yellow sweater. *Huh? A dog sweater?* But I'm glad she chose yellow, because it reminds me of the man in the yellow slicker who saved my life.

There's a brown teddy bear in the other bag; he's very soft.

What to do with him I have no idea. But Jane does.

"Oh, look! A pal for you when you get lonely."

Why would I get lonely? Jane and Brian are always around. And I guess Larry, too. But even if he wasn't here, I wouldn't get lonely for him.

The doorbell rings again, and this time it's Sandy, another of Jane's friends. She has a stuffed black cat under her arm for me.

I can't believe I'm getting presents. Back home I had sticks and bones to chew on and holes to dig. But I guess I can't dig holes or chew sticks in this house, so fuzzy little toys are the next best thing.

"Where's the Swiss cheese?" Brian calls from the kitchen.

"Wilbur ate it," somebody says.

Agneta and Hal come next, with a wild little puppy named Olof. Agneta brings homemade marrow bones. Wilbur nearly knocks me over to get next to the bag. Olof nearly knocks us both over, leaping, squealing, and spinning in the air to be the first to collect a bone. I sit nicely.

Am I the only dog in this town with manners?

We each get a bone. Wilbur goes back to the corner and devours his in about a minute. Olof decides, after all that squeaking, that he doesn't want a bone after all. He wants attention instead.

As other friends come in, they join the circle. Bob and Karen bring a rope toy. Olivia arrives with leather chewies and Emma and Conor with biscuits.

Dan staggers in last with a bag under his arm.

"Gotcha something," he says as he plops a Yankee cap on my head. "It's okay if you don't play; you can be a fan."

Dan's a cool guy.

"Nice hat," Wilbur mumbles from the corner. I go over to join him, hoping runty Olof will stay away.

"I have no idea what to do with all this stuff," I tell him.

"You'll learn."

I'm tired from all the excitement, so I doze off. I half-snore a good-bye when Wilbur and his folks leave, and several other guests follow. After everyone's gone home, I wake myself up. Brian and I sit in the living room looking at my presents.

"You got a great haul," Brian says, tossing one of the stuffed animals in the air.

That's when I remember Jane's comment about having company when I feel lonely.

What was that supposed to mean?

Chapter 18

Monday Morning Blues

It turns out that those fuzzy stuffed things are all I have for company the next morning. Larry heads out the door without even a "see ya." Jane gives me my breakfast, which includes leftover salmon that is as yummy as Mamma's. Brian comes thundering down the stairs after Jane screams at him at least three times to *get up!* When he finally does, he gulps down his food as quickly as I do and takes off carrying a huge book bag on his shoulder. On his way out, he gives me a few quick pats.

"I'll be home at five for catching practice, Hooper."

Is he trying to give me something to look forward to? Nice try.

After Jane and I walk around the block and I do my business, she scrambles around the house getting ready to leave. And that's when bad thoughts start running through my head.

No, Jane, you can't leave me here alone!

When Jane sits down to tie her running shoes, I plop myself in her lap. I know she thinks this is very cute, even though it slows her down. When she gets up, I sit on her feet. When that doesn't work, I run to the front door and block it.

Please grab my leash off the hook and take me wherever you're headed. I won't trip you! I won't slow you down! Puhleeze!

"Sorry, Hoop, I have errands." Jane sighs. "You have to stay alone for a little while, but you'll have your new toys for company until Val comes."

She reaches into the basket in the living room and pulls out the brown teddy bear.

"Remember this?" she said. "From Aunt Deborah?"

Give me a little credit here. That is not *company.* That is a wad of cotton stuffing wrapped in fake fur.

"He'll snuggle with you while I'm out, so don't chew on him."

How insulting. Does Jane really think I'd chew that thing? I'm not even going to sniff it, let alone snuggle with it. And that goes for the rest of them. They are fake friends and I'll ignore them the whole time I'm alone. I'm not a baby.

"Bye-bye, Hoopie. I'll be back soon."

Please don't go. And don't call me "Hoopie."

The door closes and locks and there is silence. No Yankee game. No clacking on computer keys. No yelling or laughter or whispers.

I wander around the house. There are no clothes on the floor in Brian's room; somebody must have cleaned up. I roll

101

around on his bed, picking up a smell or two, but it's boring. Jane's bed is neatly made, and I have a feeling she wants it to stay that way. Still, I climb up to see if it's soft and comfortable, but without any people, it isn't.

Maybe there's something going on downstairs. The kitchen counter has no chunk of cheese to swipe, but I lick up a Cheerio from the floor.

The house is quiet and no fun at all.

Is there something going on outside? I perch on Larry's kitchen chair. From there I can see the street from the window.

Oh. This is good. Traffic whizzing by. Horns blowing. No one ever blew a car horn on Mamma and George's little street. Here, people like to make music with their horns. Not very pretty music, though.

I take a drink of water from my bowl and wander over to the front door. I want to be right there when somebody comes home.

Hello? When will somebody come home?

The floor is hard and cold. I spend a minute or two chewing at an itch. I scratch my side. I sneeze.

I finally put my head down, but I can't get comfortable.

Oh, all right. I'll get that bear.

I plop down near the front door and rest my head on his belly. He makes a nice pillow. I must have drifted off to sleep because the next thing I hear is a key in the door. It's Val.

I wag and wag.

"Hooper! Wanna go to the park?"

Yes! I want to see trees and grass and flowers and I want to smell dog smells!

But I don't want to go to the dog run. Please. No dog run.

"Come on." Val smiles as she grabs my leash. "Let's go!"

As soon as we get outside, I forget being left alone. I'm free! Well, except for the leash. And the first thing I do is to pee like the other New York City boy dogs: I lift my leg. I wobble a little, but I don't fall over. I'll get better with practice!

Maybe I'll meet Wilbur. Or today will be the day I'll make a new friend. Maybe there will be a *female* friend. Yes, that would be really great. Besides Kissy, who doesn't count, I've never had a girlfriend.

The few dogs I see on the path into the park are not interested. The only creature that notices me is a *squirrel*, who smirks at me and mutters something snide that I can't quite make out.

I don't like squirrels. I didn't like squirrels back home and I discover I don't like them here, either. In fact, New York squirrels have more nerve than the ones back home in Lousiana. And they are dirtier and definitely more insulting.

I didn't really notice last time, probably because I was so busy worrying about Mel. But the path to the dog run is a squirrel highway lined with oak trees. A giant banquet of acorns covers the ground. I'm not kidding; there are at least a hundred squirrels flying around in a nut frenzy. Most of them pay no attention to people or dogs.

But one does.

Val and I are about halfway across Squirrel Highway when this particular squirrel stops burying his stupid little acorn, stands up on his hind legs, and stares right at me. He's daring me to chase him.

I'm not a growler. But this warty little creep makes me so mad that I lose it. I lunge at him, yanking the leash behind me and throwing Val off balance.

"Take it easy, Hooper!"

I can't help it! I have to get that squirrel!

But it's too late. The little creep is long gone. I can hear him snickering on a nearby branch.

And as if that isn't infuriating enough, I can see the swarm of dogs in the dog run, led by Mel.

I slow up as we get closer, and then I see an even more depressing sight: Olof is in the pack right behind Mel. Well, maybe Olof is too young to realize what a bully Mel is. Or maybe he's being sensible. If you want to make it in the dog run, I guess you have to go with the flow, just like Chrissie said. But could Chrissie really have meant putting up with somebody like Mel?

Mel sees me, and as he galumphs by, he growls, "Loser." All the dogs, including Olof, chuckle and smirk as they gallop past.

Mel is right. This is no place for me. I stop and turn around.

"You want to go home already, Hooper?" Val asks.

I'm more than ready.

As we're leaving the park, I see the beautiful bearded collie again. Wow. She is gorgeous. And there is something special about her: she is graceful and confident. She's the total opposite of me, but who knows? Maybe I have a shot with her. At least she isn't part of the swarm.

Hey, over here! Give me a look. I'm a southern boy with a lot of charm!

Nope. She doesn't see me.

Wait! She glances in my direction. Her tail wags very slowly. Is she wagging at me? I can't tell.

Who am I kidding? I'm no New York dog. I'm puny and I can't catch a ball, and I'm scared of everything, and I just wish I could go home. I'm crazy to think she'd even look at me.

When we get back, Brian and Dan are waiting for me. Brian gives me some big pats and lips my ear. Then he claps his hands and shouts, "Let's play ball!"

Chapter 19

Practice

"You *hafta* learn to play ball," Brian tells me.

"Don't pressure him," Dan says.

"We're talking twenty bucks and a chance to bust the old man's chops," Brian argues.

I'm all for busting Larry's chops, but I don't think I can really catch that stupid ball. Oh, well. If it means so much to Brian, I'll try.

"Ready?"

If you insist.

Brian puts the ball in my mouth. I lie down and start chewing it to get in the mood.

"No." Brian takes the ball out of my mouth. This time he takes a step back and leans over, letting the ball drop. It bounces off the top of my head. I wise up and move out of the way.

Next, he tries very gently bouncing the ball. "Grab it, Hooper."

Nope. The ball moves too fast.

Brian tosses it a little higher and it comes back down. I follow it and at the perfect moment I snap and chomp, but too late. My jaw shuts so hard I almost knock my teeth out. *Ouch!*

Here it comes. Snap, chomp, oops!

"One more."

Snap, chomp, *ow.*

Go ahead. Call me Thud.

Brian puts the ball down and sits beside me.

"Let me tell you a story," he begins. "Michael Jordan, the greatest basketball player who ever lived, didn't make his high school varsity team in his freshman year."

Is that a crumb under the dresser?

"Listen to me," he continues.

No, it's a dead bug.

"My point is that you have to practice. Even MJ wasn't good in the beginning."

Dan reaches into his book bag and pulls out a plastic bag of carrots.

I love carrots! Mamma used to cook them with salmon!

"Hooper, pay attention. There's a lot at stake."

Maybe, but Dan's opening the bag of carrots!

"Look at me!" Brian cries.

The ball comes my way and I dodge it. Brian sighs. "Hey, Dan, I'm hungry," he says. "Toss me one of those."

Dan tosses the carrot in the air. I leap up and catch it. *Yum!* Brian and Dan freeze in disbelief.

"Dude, that was some vertical jump," Dan gasps. "He's a natural."

"Totally!"

Brian and Dan take turns tossing pieces of carrot, and I catch them. Then the front door squeaks open and slams shut, and Larry calls out, "I'm home!"

"Up here, Dad. Dan and me are practicing catch with Hooper."

"Yeah? Bring him down here. Let's see what he can do."

Let's not.

Brian leans down and lips my ear and then whispers in it, "The key is not to panic."

"Make believe the ball is a carrot," Dan adds. "Get it?"

Then Brian grabs Dan's arm and whispers, "Dude, don't mention anything about the carrots to my dad. Hoop's not allowed to eat human food."

They trot down the stairs, ball in hand, and I follow very slowly. Why rush to be disgraced? A ball is not a carrot; it's bigger and harder, and it hurts when it hits you in the face.

And anyway, I don't feeling like showing off for Larry.

I miss the first one. Miss the second one (by a mile). Don't even try for the third one.

"Pitiful," Larry grunts. "Can he at least *chase* a ball?"

Brian shrugs. Larry throws the ball across the living room.

"Let's see! Hooper, go get the ball," Larry says, pretending that this is an exciting idea.

You know what? I could go after it. I could even bring it back and drop it at his feet. But I don't like his attitude.

"And this dog is supposed to be a retriever?" Larry snorts. "What a genetic disaster. Yankees are on in ten minutes."

He's lost interest in me. *Totally.*

Dan goes home, we troop back upstairs, and Brian turns the game on.

"Done your homework, Bri?" Larry asks.

"In study hall."

They spread out on Brian's bed and I slide under it. The game gets off to a slow start, so I fall asleep. I wake up at the bottom of the third inning when I hear Jane's voice.

"What's the score?"

"No score yet."

"Hoopie, were you a good boy today?"

Brian pipes up. "Mom, his name is Hooper. We had another catching lesson."

"Give it up," Larry scoffs.

"What difference does it make if he can catch?" Jane wants to know.

Good question!

"I mean you're not exactly All-Star material," she adds to Larry. "And I still married you."

Oh boy. She's good.

"A dog is supposed to be able to catch and fetch," Larry says sternly, looking at the screen. "But he can't do it."

"A man is supposed to be able fix the faucet, but you can't do it."

Whoa!

And Jane leaves the room.

Larry takes off a little bit later.

When I come down to the kitchen for my kibble, he has tools scattered all over the counter and is trying to fix the kitchen faucet.

Chapter 20

Willow

I don't have to stay alone in the house the next day. In the morning, Jane leashes me up for a trip to the park.

But as soon as we're outside, we see Wilbur and Ann coming along the street. Jane and Ann get into a big conversation, so Wilbur and I stretch out.

"This could take a while." Wilbur sighs.

"How was the park?"

"Okay."

Wilbur's not a big talker. You have to keep asking questions or he'll just go to sleep.

"Is that rude squirrel around?"

"You mean Howard?"

"I don't know his name."

"Yeah, you mean Howard the Mouth. He's there. Ignore him."

And that's that. Wilbur dozes off and I try very gently tugging the leash to get Jane moving. She notices and says her good-byes.

Jane takes a new path to the river walk. I'm sniffing along the way, not paying much attention to anything. Suddenly, the beautiful female bearded collie is walking straight toward us. I gulp. Am I finally going to meet this elegant creature? Will she reject me (like pretty much everyone else in this city)?

Don't blow it, Stubby. Make yourself tall. Best paw forward. I lift my head high and smile and point my tail straight up. (That's a dog signal that means, "Wow, I like you. Let's check each other out.")

She smiles! Jane and her mom are walking at a regular pace, and we're straining at our leashes to get closer.

"Hooper! Are you wanting to play with that pretty dog?"

Gee, Jane, how could you tell?

It seems like forever, but we finally meet up and wag madly. Then we sniff and she rolls over on her back playfully.

She's flirting with me!

Her mom says, "Goodness! Willow sure likes your dog."

Willow rolls and jumps on me. Our tails are wagging so hard we keep bumping butts. Then we run in little circles and our leashes get all tangled.

Jane has a brilliant idea. "Let's go to the lower run," she suggests. "If it's empty, they can play."

Jane and the other lady walk along while we try to gallop ahead, but until we get to the run, we can barely manage a trot. Leashes are awful!

Sure enough, we arrive at another dog run. Mel isn't there. In fact, no dogs are there at all. After we get through the double gates, we're set free.

Willow and I run in a big circle. Sometimes I chase her, and then suddenly she spins around and chases me. Her beautiful silky hair feathers out in all directions. We run and roll. We dance up on our hind legs. We sniff and slurp from a fountain for dogs. (A fountain for dogs—I've never seen anything like it!)

After all that, we pant and wag and smile. To be polite, I formally introduce myself.

"I'm Hooper."

"I'm Willow."

"Hi, Willow." (I wish I could come up with something clever, but I'm too nervous.)

"Are you new in town?"

"Yes." I can feel myself blushing. (Yes, we blush, but it's invisible under our coats.) "Do you come to this park a lot?"

"Sometimes."

Honestly, I'm so crazy about her I don't know what to say next, so I chase her again. The whole park is a blur as we run in circles.

"Hooper!"

"Willow!"

"Time to go!" Jane and the other mom call out.

We both hang our heads while they leash us, and we leave the run as slowly as we can. When it's time to go in different directions, we stare at each other, resisting the tugs at the other ends of our leashes.

"Bye," I whisper.

"See ya," she whispers back.

I look over my shoulder at her and she's smiling back at me.

When we get to Squirrel Highway, I don't even remember to look for Howard. I'm much too busy thinking about Willow.

Chapter 21

Another Storm

I'm so happy I could wag my tail fast enough to fly. As we walk back from *my first date ever*, Jane promises that Willow and I will have more dates.

Not even Big Larry can take my joy away from me.

But he doesn't try. That evening he ignores me, which is fine. Brian has a lot of homework, but he watches the game on TV with the sound off. I curl up on the bed and dream about my next date with Willow.

After a while I start dreaming about a big roast beef bone instead. I slip off Brian's bed and I head toward the kitchen.

Larry is still trying to fix the faucet. Jane is leaning on the counter next to him and handing him tools. I don't think they notice me.

I stick my nose in my bowl. Empty. No juicy roast beef

bone. Rats. I drink a little water instead.

I hear Jane say my name. And then Larry grumbles something. I don't catch the beginning of it. But it ends with "can't even bark."

"He's just a puppy," Jane says softly.

Larry grunts.

"I know you miss Hammer. I do, too."

Larry doesn't say anything.

"Brian was ready for a new dog, Larry. And all those dogs lost their homes. . . . We did a good thing."

Larry picks up a wrench, then puts it down again.

Jane's voice is very soft. "Open your heart a little."

She hands him the right wrench.

Larry doesn't say anything. And for some reason I don't want to let them know I've been listening. I slip out as quietly as I can, trying not to let my toenails click on the floor.

It begins to drizzle while Brian is working on his homework. Jane and I go out for a really quick walk, which is fine by me. I still hate getting even a little damp. There is no way I could forget the storm in Lake Charles.

Jane turns out the light in their room, and Brian and I decide to watch a little nighttime television. Soon there is a lot of snoring coming from the direction of Jane and Larry's bed. Then I realize there's another noise. It's a snore farther in the distance, or so I think at first. Maybe it's Other Larry snoring next door. Or Wilbur. But this snoring isn't snoring; it's rumbling I've heard before. It's the sound of *thunder.*

I jump off the bed in search of a hiding place. I stay low to the ground.

"Relax, Hooper, it's just rain," Brian assures me.

Just rain? If you'd seen what I've seen, you'd know better. There's no such thing as *just rain*. I dive under the bed, but I can hear the rumble and cracks getting closer. Soon they'll be on top of us. *No! Not again!*

Brian peers under the bed. "It's okay. Come on out."

It's not okay. Believe me. I know.

The television goes black and the hall light turns off. At first, Brian thinks it's the remote and goes over to the set to turn the TV back on. He tosses the remote on the floor and pulls up the shade to look out the window.

"Crud, we have a power failure."

There's a flash of lightning. The storm is on our roof. I start to pant.

Brian reaches down and pulls me out and lifts me onto his bed. We snuggle under his Yankee blanket.

Crack! Crash!

That bang sounds like it's *right inside this room*! It's nearly as loud as the one that exploded the old cypress tree in Mamma's yard!

I lurch from Brian's arms and trip off the bed, hitting my head on the floor and knocking over a pile of books in the process. I race into the bathroom as fast as I can. I don't know why I pick the bathroom. I just find myself in there, and I jump into the tub and hide behind the shower curtain. That way I

117

can't see the storm and it can't see me.

Brian runs into the bathroom and sits on the edge of the tub. *Close the curtain!*

"Hooper, it's okay. You're safe here. The storm can't get inside."

Oh, yes it can!

Brian rubs my head and whispers over and over, "Don't worry. You're safe with me."

The thunder explodes, and even though the bathroom has no window, I can see the lightning turning Brian's room from night to day.

"Hooper, this is New York City. We don't have storms that knock over buildings. This house is solid stone. It was built over a hundred years ago. We're not on a gulf; we're on a river that's half a mile from here."

Leave me alone. You have no idea what you're talking about. I turn away from him.

"Hooper, I would *never* let anything bad happen to you. I swear."

I know you're trying to help, but it won't work.

"Shh. Listen! It's already passing through."

It *is* getting quieter. But sometimes storms try to trick you. I remember how it got quieter and peaceful last time, and I was sure I'd be back home soon. Then it started right up again.

But this storm isn't tricky like that. We wait right there in the tub until the only sound we can hear is the distant whisper of the rain.

Hmm. I *was* scared, but now I'm getting mad.

In fact, the storm makes me furious. After all the struggles I've been through, I'm not going to put up with this anymore. No storm has the right to do this to me. Brian isn't afraid. Larry is still snoring; the storm didn't even wake him up!

Hey! I don't have to be hiding anymore. Hear me?

And right then and there, I let go a great big bark.

Jane and Larry come flying into the bathroom.

Brian is thrilled!

"Mom! Dad! Hooper can bark!"

And then something happens that I wasn't expecting at all. Larry says, "Atta boy! You tell that storm what you think of it!"

And I bark again, good and loud.

Now, I can't say for sure whether my bark did it or not, but the hall light pops back on and the television, too!

Nobody gets mad that Brian and I were watching the television. Just the opposite. Everyone goes back to bed smiling.

I must have given that storm a shock; the next morning the sun is shining.

Chapter 22

Mel

After breakfast, Larry decides to take me for a walk instead of Mom or Val. Even though he was friendlier last night, I'm uneasy. I want him to like me, but if anything goes wrong (again), he might decide that he's not keeping me after all. (Hey, dogs remember threats like that.)

"Take your ball, Hooper," he tells me.

We're already getting off to a bad start. I carry the ball in my mouth, but I have no intention of playing catch.

When we get to Squirrel Highway, Howard mumbles, "Look whooze here," but he's busy burying an acorn, so his tiny brain is occupied. Just when I think we've made it past him, he finishes his big task and yells, "Hey, moron, whatchoo got in your mouth? A dog pacifier?"

Naturally I can't answer; I have a tennis ball in my mouth.

"Whatzamatter? Can't think of anything to say?"

I put the ball down gently and mosey toward him. He stands on those little hind legs and stares. He's daring me again.

I could bark and scare him good, but I do something better. I dig up his crummy acorn and send it flying into the air!

"*Hey!* Whadyadoo that for?" Howard cries, outraged.

And because I'm polite, I just smile and pick up my ball and go on my way.

I'm feeling pretty darned proud of myself—that is, until I look over into the dog run.

There's Mel, tormenting an overweight corgi mix who's straining at the back of the swarm. I feel for him; I know what it's like.

"Keep up or step off, pygmy!" he roars.

I sit down and Larry sighs. "Not up to it yet, huh, Hoop?" he says. And he waits with me until I see Willow in the run; she's standing off to the side by herself. My heart thumps with anticipation. I *have* to go in and see her!

Larry looks stunned when I tug at the leash. He follows me into the run. Looking very puzzled, he unhooks my leash.

"Willow! Hey!"

And she floats right over, smiling and wagging.

"Hooper! Hi!"

We dance and sniff and roll.

The whole world is happy and warm, until Mel stomps over.

"Gimme your tennis ball, sissy," he hisses, sending a spray of drool in my face. The swarm stops and waits for me to drop the ball at Mel's enormous dirty paws.

Willow looks at me with panic in her eyes. Everyone does. Even Larry.

I sit down and hold the ball tightly in my jaw. I look at Mel and don't move. Mel is confused.

"You deaf?" he screams, but his voice isn't as deep and certain.

Of course I can't answer, because that means dropping the ball. So I sit up very straight and still, waiting for him to make his next move.

The whole dog run is frozen. Nobody dares twitch.

Mel moves toward me slowly and I can hear his chest rumbling. His growl is deep and ominous; he's so close I can smell his rancid breath. He's seconds away from ripping my throat out.

I don't budge.

He crouches, preparing to spring, when Willow slides between us and presses her nose right into Mel's monster face.

In the calmest voice, Willow says, "Knock it off, Mel. You're an overbearing slob and you're done here."

There is another frightening pause. And then Mel actually takes a step backward.

"We'll see," he sputters.

He lumbers around the run, waiting for his swarm to follow, but nobody does. Every dog in the run stands stock still, unblinking. Mouths hang open and drool puddles into mud. Frisbees and balls are deserted. Even the humans are paralyzed. Mel looks over his shoulder at an empty space.

Willow smiles at me. Doesn't she realize the *hugeness* of what she's done? "He's such a jerk." She sighs. "He made everyone's life miserable."

"But Willow, where did you get the courage to go right into his face?"

"From you, Hooper."

"From me?" I gasp.

"You were a hero. You didn't give up your tennis ball. And you were a perfect gentleman about it."

Secretly I thank One-Eye. But now I'm so full of joy and amazement at the whole thing that I sit down beside Willow, as close as I can get. She nuzzles my neck and we sit there together, right in Riverside Park. Mel's dad comes to leash him up and take him home, and we don't even look at him as he passes by.

After a while, Willow's mom comes to get her leash on, and then Larry comes for me. Larry is so excited, he can barely get his words out.

"Hooper, you were so brave out there. That dog is three times as big as you with a head like Mount Rushmore!"

I don't know who Mount Rushmore is, but I assume he has a big head.

"And the way you kept your cool! You were uh-uh-uhmazing!" Larry is stammering. "I can't think of any dog in the world who could have handled that monster better!"

Hmmm. Not even Hammer?

"Where did you get your moxie?"

My what?

As we're going, Olof charges up to the fence.

"Hooper!" he squeals. "This run is totally yours now!"

"Thanks, but I don't want it."

"Please, come play with us!"

"Later, Olof. Now I'm going home."

And that's when it hits me. Chrissie was right. She found me a new family, and now, after a few days, I'm getting the hang of them. I have a new home! Jane is my new mom; she has been since the first. And Brian—he's just kind of like a big overgrown puppy himself. I guess that makes him my brother.

And Larry—well, he isn't Dad yet. But I guess it's okay for him just to be Larry.

As we go through Squirrel Highway, Howard is nowhere to be found.

I guess news travels fast on the Upper West Side of Manhattan, because when we get to Other Larry and Ann's house, Wilbur is on the stoop waiting to congratulate me. He actually wags his tail a little.

"Mel's going to another park from now on," he says with a half-smile. "Cool move, dude."

And Other Larry adds, "Hooper, for a southern guy, you got New York nerve."

When we get home, Larry acts out the whole scene for Mom and again for Brian when he comes home from school. He goes through it all again the next day when Val arrives and at least four times on the phone.

Each time the story gets a little bigger and less believable. I don't care; when no one is looking, Larry gives me a hunk of ham and a wedge of cheese.

The whole night, everyone keeps smiling and patting me. To tell the truth, I don't know why. All I did was mind my manners and go with the flow. Just like Chrissie told me to.

Chapter 23

A Few Surprises

I wake up the next morning and can hardly wait for Brian to get up. In fact, I tug at his covers and lick his face to get him going. I admit it; I want to go to the park. While he's pulling on a T-shirt, I root through my toy basket and find a fat rope with knots on each end. It smells pretty interesting. I pull it out and chew on one of the knots.

Then I get tired of waiting for Brian, who's digging around in a pile of clothes for some jeans. I charge down the stairs with the rope dangling from my mouth. Mom and Larry are having breakfast.

"Hey, Hooper, bring that over here," Larry shouts with a mouthful of toast. I bolt over and give it to him.

"Good boy, Hoop. Now grab one end and pull!"

What the heck is he talking about?

Larry wiggles the rope in front of my face and says, "Grab it! Come on!"

So I do and he starts pulling it away. Since he seems to want the rope so badly, I drop it and roll over on my back.

"Oh, Hooper, don't be scared. Let's *play*!"

Larry dangles the rope in front of my face again. I bite it and he pulls, more gently this time. I pull back just a little. He yells, "That's it!" So I pull a little harder and then Larry gives the rope a big yank and I slip and flop over.

Mom snorts behind her newspaper. Larry looks at her indignantly.

"Give him a chance, Jane. He's still learning."

"Oh, really?"

Mom is holding the paper up so Larry can't see her face. But I notice her big smile.

"It's okay, Hoop," Larry says. "Get up and pull some more." So I grab the end of the rope and pull really hard, and the next thing I know Larry and I are having a tug of war. He pretends to growl and I growl back.

And Larry says, "Hooper, you're turning into a real dog!"

Mom rustles her newspaper and folds it up. "We've got to get Brian out of the way this morning," she says to Larry.

"We'll make Brian take Hooper to the park," Larry answers. "You can do that, right, Hooper?"

Sure thing!

When Brian comes stumbling downstairs at last, still

looking half asleep, Mom tells him to take me out after he finishes breakfast. So off we go to Riverside Park.

Naturally, Howard is in the park with his grubby friends. Will he be more polite now that I've shown him who was boss? Of course not. This is New York, after all.

I show my teeth as a little reminder.

"Yeah? You're all teeth and no bite," he shouts. "You can't even bark."

I pause and look at him very calmly.

"Thatz what I thought." Howard cackles. "You're a no-nerve ninny."

I don't react, so he moves closer.

"I know field mice who've got more guts than you."

Apparently he isn't keeping up with local gossip. I wait until he's inches from my face. Guess what, chump?

WOOF!

Howard can move fast when he has to. All I see is a gray streak shooting up the nearest tree.

"What?" I shout up. "Leaving without a good-bye?"

"Aah, big deal." He shrugs. "So you can bark."

There's no way to shut down a New Yorker. But I notice he stays up in the tree.

The big run is almost empty and Mel is nowhere to be seen. Neither is Willow, sad to say. But I'm sure I'll see her another day, and that's enough to make me happy, for now.

After a while we head back home. When we come in from the park, the living room is full of people. I see Mom and

Larry, Val, Other Larry, Ann, Dan, and lots more people I haven't met yet. They all yell, "*Surprise!* Happy birthday!"

Brian looks totally shocked, and very, very happy.

While the guests hug and give Brian gifts, I join Wilbur and Olof at the foot of the buffet table.

"Mom! Gimme some ham!" Olof squeals.

Wilbur and I look at each other. Olof is such a kid.

"I'm gonna grab a nap." Wilbur yawns. "Wake me when they're giving out food." And he wanders off into the corner.

I sit next to the buffet table and wait patiently. Being patient has many rewards. One by one, people come over and give me bits of cheese and salmon and chicken.

Everyone gathers in the living room to sing "Happy Birthday" to Brian. Then there are lots more hugs and somebody yells, "Speech!"

Brian smiles and raises his soda glass. He almost looks like a grown-up.

"Thanks for the cool surprise. This is a perfect birthday because we were so sad when Hammer died, and since we got Hooper, we're a happy family again."

"Hear, hear!" Larry yells.

Brian has something behind his back in the hand that isn't holding a glass. He holds it up and grins.

"And I think this is the perfect moment for *another* surprise. Hooper, get ready. You're going to *catch*!"

"Now that I'd like to see," Larry says, not in a mean way, but with a touch of doubt.

Brian tosses the ball a little too hard, and it bounces off the wall and rolls under the sofa.

Ball one. I've learned something from watching all those baseball games on TV.

His second pitch is in the strike zone, but I miss it. Lots of people in the room groan. Larry bites his lip.

Strike one.

Two wild pitches in a row and a perfect slider follow.

Full count.

This is the moment of truth. I can hear the Yankees announcer:

"It's the bottom of the ninth, the Yanks and the Sox are tied three all, two outs, full count on Hooper. And the pitch—"

Brian tosses the tennis ball in the air. I take a breath and suddenly everything is moving in slow motion.

Brian's pitch is high and outside. I adjust. I leap. I snap. I chomp. I feel the sweet yellow fuzz of the tennis ball on my tongue and I sink my teeth in it.

Nothing happens. No one makes a sound.

Larry is so surprised that a piece of salmon on a cracker falls right out of his mouth, and he doesn't make a fuss when I snatch it up and eat it.

Then Brian screams, *"Ladies and gentlemen, we have a winner!"*

And everyone starts shouting at once.

"Getouttahere!"

"Did you see that, Larry?"

"Hooper caught the ball!"

"And it was a lousy pitch!"

"*See?* And you thought he'd never do it, oh ye of little faith."

"You owe me. Fork it over."

"Give the Hoopster a shout-out. *Yay!*"

I don't believe it myself. *I caught a fly ball!*

"Hooper, you're more than a New York dog: You're a *Yankee!*" Larry says, and gives me a big pat on my head.

Then Larry reaches into his pocket and pulls out twenty dollars.

"Now this is money well spent," he says, handing it to Brian.

When the last of the party guests have left, Larry, Brian, and I plop down on the living room sofa. Mom starts cleaning up.

Larry says, "Sit down for a minute, Jane. We'll help you clean up, but first let's relax for a few."

I thump my tail, hoping she'll join us, and she does.

"How'd you like Brian's birthday party, Hooper?"

I thump even harder.

"It was a great surprise," Brian says happily. "I can't believe you guys kept it a secret."

"Couldn't have done it without Hooper," Larry says proudly.

And that's when I know that Larry isn't Larry anymore.

He's Dad.

And I'm not Jimmy anymore.

I'm Hooper.

"Bri, can you give me a hand clearing the dishes?" Mom says.

"You bet!"

Dad pats the spot next to him on the sofa. I squiggle over.

"Go get a toy," he whispers. "Let's play."

I have a real family now. It's warm in the room, and in this moment it is warm in my heart. My family is together and we are all happy. The terrible storm of long ago is a distant memory. I'm safe and I'm home and I'm loved.

Meet Hooper, the real-life dog who inspired this story.

Napping after breakfast

Story time at the library

All dressed up for Brian's birthday party

First day in New York City

First toy

"I hate baths."

Baseball practice

Reading with Emma and Conor

Afterword

From Hooper's point of view, the storm was a scary adventure with a happy ending.

Many people were far less fortunate. Hurricane Katrina was one of our nation's worst disasters; an estimated 1,800 people died and 300,000 were left homeless. Even more people lost their jobs because so many businesses and farms could not recover from the damage Katrina caused.

The hurricane hit the Gulf of Mexico coastline in August 2005 with such force that parts of Louisiana, Mississippi, and Alabama were left in ruins. New Orleans sustained the worst damage because the levees built to protect the city could not withstand the pressure of the waves and winds. As a result, whole sections were submerged in more than twenty feet of water, forcing residents to seek refuge wherever they could.

Televisions around the world showed images of the devastation left in the wake of the hurricane; the suffering was heartbreaking. Many citizens here and abroad supported organizations to help the survivors with medical care, food, water, housing, and other basic necessities.

Animal rescue volunteers saved and relocated thousands of abandoned and lost pets, farm animals, and wildlife.

The toll on the Gulf Coast was (and continues to be) enormous, but the love and compassion so many of us feel for the victims will stay in our hearts forever.

Acknowledgments

There would be no Hooper without Labs4rescue, the volunteer organization that matched him with our family. In particular, Katie Roush, the actual matchmaker in Lake Charles, Louisiana, and Mindy Franklin Levine in New York City, who provided resources for Hoop and boundless kindness and encouragement for me.

And there would be no Hooper book without HarperCollins, with a big shout-out to Alyson Day, who edited with a gentle hand and a great sense of humor.

Big thanks to my BFF, Deborah Aal Stoff, who is the only person in the world who can boss me around and get away with it.

I'm blessed with great pals: Danielle, Olivia, Sandy, Diane, Maxine, Karen, and Carla.

And I'm even more blessed with a near-perfect son, Brian.

And, of course, the real Larry, the love of my life, who is not as grumpy as he appears in this book.